P9-AEX-743

ISSUES THAT CONCERN YOU

Artificial Ingredients

Lauri S. Scherer, *Book Editor*

GREENHAVEN PRESS
A part of Gale, Cengage Learning

GALE
CENGAGE Learning·

Detroit • New York • San Francisco • New Haven, Conn • Waterville, Maine • London

Elizabeth Des Chenes, *Director, Publishing Solutions*

© 2013 Greenhaven Press, a part of Gale, Cengage Learning

Gale and Greenhaven Press are registered trademarks used herein under license.

For more information, contact:
Greenhaven Press
27500 Drake Rd.
Farmington Hills, MI 48331-3535
Or you can visit our Internet site at gale.cengage.com

For product information and technology assistance, contact us at

Gale Customer Support, 1-800-877-4253
For permission to use material from this text or product, submit all requests online at www.cengage.com/permissions

Further permissions questions can be e-mailed to permissionrequest@cengage.com

Articles in Greenhaven Press anthologies are often edited for length to meet page requirements. In addition, original titles of these works are changed to clearly present the main thesis and to explicitly indicate the author's opinion. Every effort is made to ensure that Greenhaven Press accurately reflects the original intent of the authors. Every effort has been made to trace the owners of copyrighted material.

Cover image © Gunter Nezhoda/Shutterstock.com.

LIBRARY OF CONGRESS CATALOGING-IN-PUBLICATION DATA

Artificial ingredients / Lauri S. Scherer, book editor.
    p. cm. -- (Issues that concern you)
Summary: "Artificial Ingredients: This series provides readers with information on topics of current interest. Focusing on important social issues, each anthology examines its subject in a variety of ways, from personal accounts to factual articles"-- Provided by publisher.
  Includes bibliographical references and index.
  ISBN 978-0-7377-6284-6 (hardback)
  1. Food additives. 2. Food substitutes. 3. Artificial foods. I. Scherer, Lauri S., editor of compilation.
  TX553.A3A78 2012
  641.3'08--dc23
                                               2012029193

Printed in the United States of America
1 2 3 4 5 6 7 16 15 14 13 12

CONTENTS

Introduction   5

1. Artificial Ingredients Pose a Serious Health Threat   10
   Kristen Wartman

2. Consumers Exaggerate the Health Threat from
   Artificial Ingredients   17
   Harriet Hall

3. Artificial Sweeteners Are Safe   25
   Susan B. Roberts

4. Artificial Sweeteners Are Very Dangerous   32
   Joseph Mercola

5. It Is Difficult to Determine the Safety of
   Artificial Ingredients   41
   Marion Nestle, as told to the San Francisco Chronicle

6. Artificial Ingredients Cause Behavioral
   Problems in Children   46
   David W. Schab and Michael F. Jacobson

7. The Link Between Artificial Ingredients and
   Behavioral Problems Is Unproven   52
   Rob Johnston

8. Artificial Food Colorings Should Be Banned   58
   Center for Science in the Public Interest

9. Artificial Food Colorings Should Not Be Banned   66
   Gardiner Harris

10. Bisphenol A Should Be Banned   70
    Dianne Feinstein

11. Bisphenol A Should Not Be Banned   76
   Lisa De Pasquale

12. Consumers Want Products with Natural and
   Organic Ingredients   81
   Carolyn Dimitri and Catherine Greene

13. Consumers May Not Want Alternatives to
   Artificial Ingredients   87
   Taryn Luna

Appendix

    What You Should Know About Artificial Ingredients   92
    What You Should Do About Artificial Ingredients   95

Organizations to Contact   100

Bibliography   105

Index   109

Picture Credits   114

Artificial ingredients are widely used in food production—the company Earth Fare estimates that more than 90 percent of all packaged foods sold in conventional grocery stores contain at least some artificial ingredients, such as hydrogenated oils, food colorings, or preservatives. Artificial ingredients are popular because they offer a "have your cake and eat it, too" approach to food. They help products achieve an unnaturally long shelf life, meeting people's need for the food they buy to stay good for a long time. Some kinds of artificial ingredients help products taste good yet have fewer calories, meeting consumer desire to diet without sacrificing the foods or tastes they crave. Others help foods appear the way people think they should: brightly colored, cakey, powdery, or otherwise properly textured or colored.

Yet increasing attention has been paid to the threat that may be posed by loading foods up with elements generated in the chemistry lab. Two artificial ingredients that have particularly claimed the spotlight in recent years include high fructose corn syrup and partially hydrogenated vegetable oil (also known as "trans fat").

High fructose corn syrup is a kind of sugar made from corn. Popular because it can be made very cheaply and is stable in a wide variety of foods, high fructose corn syrup is consumed in large amounts by many Americans. In 2010 the US Department of Agriculture reported that Americans consume about thirty-five pounds of high fructose corn syrup per year. The *Washington Post* reports that on average, Americans ingest about twelve teaspoonsful of the stuff each day, while teenagers and other sugar-loving segments of society eat even more. In addition to contributing to epidemic rates of obesity, some studies suggest that corn syrup contains mercury, which harms brain development and could cause cancer. "Because it's cheap, consumption of high-fructose corn syrup has gone up so much in recent decades and has become one of the main sources of calories in our diet,"[1] says Frank Hu, professor of nutrition at the Harvard School of Public Health. Negative press and pressure from consumer advocacy groups has led many manufacturers to remove high fructose corn syrup from their products, though it is being reintroduced to many foods under the more benign name "corn sugar."

High fructose corn syrup joins other artificial ingredients, such as partially hydrogenated oils, or trans fats, that have become known for their link to serious and potentially fatal diseases. Trans fats are created when hydrogen is added to vegetable oil to make it less prone to spoilage, which helps keep processed cakes, cookies, and other foods on shelves longer, and to avoid having a heavy, greasy taste. But trans fats have been shown to critically raise so-called bad cholesterol levels, which in turn can lead to heart disease, which the Centers of Disease Control and Prevention reports is the number one cause of death among Americans. Trans fats have also been linked to Alzheimer's disease, breast cancer, diabetes, infertility, and other serious diseases and disorders.

The United States government maintains that trans fats are safe and thus has not federally banned them, although they do require packaged foods that contain trans fats to be labeled as such. No restrictions are placed on the use of trans fats in restaurant dishes, however, which troubles analysts at the Public Health Law Center. "Americans are purchasing meals in restaurants on an increasingly frequent basis," they note, "but because restaurant foods are exempt from federal nutrition labeling requirements, consumers have no consistent way of determining which restaurant foods contain high levels of artificial trans fat and no practical means of avoiding them."[2]

In the wake of federal nonaction, some states have taken action on their own. In 2008, California became the first—and as of 2012, only—state to ban restaurants from using trans fats in food (although Puerto Rico, a US territory, banned them in 2007). Although bans have been considered in Connecticut, Florida, Hawaii, Illinois, Maryland, Massachusetts, Michigan, Mississippi, New Hampshire, New Jersey, New Mexico, New York, Oregon, Rhode Island, South Carolina, Tennessee, Vermont, and Virginia, no other state government has yet banned them.

PARTIALLY HYDROGENATED COTTONSEED OIL, ...
... WITH TBHQ AND CITRIC ACID ADDED TO ...
... GH FRUCTOSE CORN SYRUP, CONTAINS TW...
... OOD STARCH – MODIFIED, SKIM MILK, LE...
... YROPHOSPHATE, MONOCALCIUM PHOSPH...
... ERIDES, SALT, SORBIC ACID (TO PRESER...
... RTIFICIAL FLAVORS, PROPYLENE GLYCOL M...
... R, SOY LECITHIN, XANTHAN GUM, AGAR, NU...

A list of ingredients on a package of snack food shows several artificial ingredients. More than 90 percent of all prepackaged foods are estimated to contain at least some artificial ingredients.

Local municipalities have enacted laws, too. In December 2006, New York City became the first city to ban trans fats. It prohibits all food vendors from selling foods that contain trans fats. The ban was so successful that similar initiatives have been passed in Philadelphia; Boston; Cambridge, Massachusetts; Stamford, Connecticut; Montgomery County, Maryland, and several New York counties. A couple of European countries have enacted bans as well: Denmark banned them in 2003, Switzerland in 2008, and medical organizations in the United Kingdom have repeatedly called for the British government to enact such a ban. The Public Health Law Center estimates that the Danish ban has helped Danes ingest less than a gram of trans fat per day, compared with Americans, who as of 2005 were ingesting an average of 5.8 grams per day (according to the Food and Drug Administration), despite the American Heart Association's recommendation that people ingest no more than 2 grams per day. The Center for Science in the Public Interest applauds these bans but points out that such bans protect just 18 percent of the American population. In their opinion, more bans are needed: they estimate a complete ban on trans fats in the United States would save approximately fifty thousand lives each year.

Opponents of the bans differ on this, however. Critics complain that trans fat bans are unnecessary, a hysterical overreaction to a nonproblem. "While trans fat may not be health food, it's not a poison warranting a government ban," argues Richard Berman, executive director of the Center for Consumer Freedom. "Trans fat is just the food scare du jour, having taken saturated fat's place as the dietary demon that must be exorcised."[3] Others suggest that bans suffocate local businesses and place undue restrictions on interstate commerce, complicating chain restaurants' ability to provide their franchises with the same products, regardless of what city, county, or state in which they operate. Still others resent any efforts to ban food, saying that people have the right to decide for themselves what to consume. "It's true the body doesn't 'need' trans fat," argues Berman.

> Then again, the human body doesn't 'need' fried chicken, chocolate or wine. That's not an argument for forcibly banning them. So what's next? Ice cream? Birthday cake? Why don't we outlaw skydiving? It's not like anyone does it to commute to work, and it's not exactly the world's safest form of recreation. If the government's going to be our nanny, there's no reason to limit it to bans on food only. . . . On the other hand, we could also envision an America that treats its citizens like responsible adults.[4]

Whether to ban artificial food ingredients like high fructose corn syrup and trans fat are just a few of the questions considered in *Issues That Concern You: Artificial Ingredients*. Readers will consider opposing perspectives on artificial ingredients' status, health threat, and other concerns surrounding this increasingly relevant topic.

Notes

1. Quoted in China Millman, "Nutrition Fact Check: High-Fructose Corn Syrup," *Pittsburgh Post-Gazette*, April 30, 2012. www.post-gazette.com/stories/news/health/nutrition-fact -check-high-fructose-corn-syrup-633674.
2. Public Health Law Center, "Trans Fat Bans: Policy Options for Eliminating the Use of Artificial Trans Fats in Restaurants," January 2009. http://phlc.stylefish.com/sites/default/files /resources/phlc-policy-trans-fat.pdf.
3. Richard Berman, "Should Government Ban Trans Fats? Bans Are Hysterical—but Not Funny," *San Francisco Chronicle*, October 18, 2006. www.sfgate.com/cgi-bin/article.cgi?f =/c/a/2006/10/18/EDG6PKDVPSl.DTL.
4. Berman, "Should Government Ban Trans Fats?"

ONE

Artificial Ingredients Pose a Serious Health Threat

Kristen Wartman

In the following viewpoint Kristen Wartman warns that people ingest or come into contact with thousands of artificial ingredients that pose a serious threat to their health. She discusses the toxic effects of multiple ingredients that are in foods and items largely regarded as safe. Since many chemicals are untested, Wartman warns that they have an unpredictable effect on health but likely contribute to cancer, disease, infertility, obesity, learning disorders, and other problems. In Wartman's opinion, governmental regulatory agencies need to do a better job of testing and regulating artificial ingredients. She thinks they need to let people know what substances are dangerous and make it more difficult for companies to use such substances.

Wartman is a food writer whose articles have appeared in the *Huffington Post* and on the Grist website.

Chemicals and additives found in the food supply and other consumer products are making headlines regularly as more and more groups raise concern over the safety of these substances. In a statement released this week [in April 2011], the American Academy of Pediatrics (AAP) asked for reform to the Toxic Substances Control Act of 1976. The group is particularly concerned about the effects these substances have on children and babies.

Last month, the U.S. Food & Drug Administration (FDA) held hearings on the safety of food dyes but failed to make a definitive ruling. The most recent study on Bisphenol-A (BPA) added to growing doubts about its safety; but the FDA's stance on it remains ambiguous. Meanwhile, in 2010, the Government Accountability Office (GAO) reported that the FDA is not ensuring the safety of many chemicals.

Constant Exposure to Toxic Substances

Yet while the FDA stalls and hedges on the safety of these substances, Americans are exposed to untested combinations of food additives, dyes, preservatives, and chemicals on a daily basis. Indeed, for the vast majority of Americans consuming industrial foods, a veritable chemical cocktail enters their bodies every day and according to the GAO report, "FDA is not systematically ensuring the continued safety of current GRAS substances."

The term GRAS refers to "generally regarded as safe," the moniker the FDA uses to regulate food additives, dyes, and preservatives. The trouble is, this system is not effective. Dr. Michael Hansen, a senior scientist at Consumers Union, said in an interview that many additives in our food supply are never even tested. That's because the GRAS designation is a voluntary process—instead of being required to register food additives, companies can notify the FDA about their product, but only if they so choose. Hansen added that even for those additives considered GRAS, he didn't have much faith in the designation.

Swimming in a "Chemical Soup"

So just how many of these largely untested and unregulated chemicals is the average American consuming every day? As of yet, no study has determined this number nor has looked at what the effects of the various combinations might be. But according to the Is It In Us? website, there are 80,000 chemicals in commerce and the site says that, "No one is ever exposed to a single chemical,

From breakfast through lunch, snacks, and dinner, a person may consume more than sixty food additives and artificial ingredients each day.

but to a chemical soup, the ingredients of which may interact to cause unpredictable health effects."

There are only a few studies that evaluate the combined effects of food additives. One 2006 study published in *Toxicology Science* concludes that the combination of several common additives appears to have a neurotoxic effect: "Although the use of single food additives at their regulated concentrations is believed to be relatively safe in terms of neuronal development, their combined effects remain unclear." Of the four additives looked at, only one is now banned in the U.S., while the rest remain in the foods on our grocery store shelves. In a 2000 study, researchers looked at the combination of four major food additives or a mixture of six typical artificial food colors and found indications of toxicity in both.

And perhaps the most alarming study dates back to 1976 from the *Journal of Food Science*. In this study, young rats were fed a low-fiber diet along with sodium cyclamate, FD&C Red No. 2, and polyoxyethylene (20) sorbitan monostearate individually and in combination. While the study found that any one of the three food additives given individually had little negative effect, the combination of all three additives resulted in weight loss and the death of all test animals within 14 days. Sodium cyclamate is an artificial sweetener now banned in the U.S., but FD&C Red No. 2, a food dye, and polyoxyethylene (20) sorbitan monostearate, an emulsifier, are still in regular use in the food supply, according to the FDA's website.

No Chance to Detox

BPA, another regularly used chemical, has raised a number of concerns. The most recent study found that when participants switched to a diet with minimal amounts of canned foods or plastic food packaging, urinary levels of BPA decreased by more than 60 percent after just three days. According to the Centers for Disease Control (CDC), nearly all Americans have detectable levels of BPA in their bodies, which has been linked to breast and prostrate cancer, infertility, early puberty in girls, obesity, and ADHD [attention-deficit/hyperactivity disorder]. This study indicates how quickly the body will excrete BPA if given the opportunity, but here's the key: The body must be given the opportunity to do so. Many Americans don't take three-day fresh food breaks from a diet based largely on packaged and processed foods.

What's more, BPA is just one of the chemical compounds with potentially harmful effects entering into our systems.

A Closer Look

Based on the anecdotal information I see in my clients' food journals, people eating processed and packaged foods are taking in exorbitant amounts of artificial ingredients and additives. Typically, a client will say something like, "I eat a bowl of cereal with low-fat milk, have yogurt for a snack, and a Subway sandwich for lunch." While this sounds relatively harmless, here's what it might actually look like based on some popular "health food" items:

- One serving of Kellogg's Fiber Plus Antioxidants Berry Yogurt Crunch contains more than 13 different additives, preservatives, and food dyes, including Red 40 and Blue 1, which are known to cause allergic reactions in some people and mutations leading to cancer in lab animals. It also contains BHT, monoglycerides, and cellulose gum. In addition, conventional milk often contains residues of artificial bovine growth hormones, known endocrine disruptors as well as antibiotics used in industrial milk production.
- Dannon Light & Fit Peach yogurt contains more than 11 different additives including Red 40, aspartame, potassium sorbate, sucralose, and acesulfame potassium.
- A Subway sandwich of turkey and cheese on nine-grain bread with fat-free honey mustard, peppers, and pickles contains more than 40 different additives, preservatives, and dyes. The pickles and peppers have Yellow 5 and polysorbate 80, the bread has 10 different additives including dough conditioners, DATEM [diacetyl tartaric acid ester of mono- and diglycerides], and sodium stearoyl lactylate, and the turkey contains 10 additives as well.

The person in this example has consumed more than 60 food additives eating breakfast, a small snack, and lunch alone, to say nothing of dinner, dessert, further snacking, and drinks. Consumers Union's Dr. Hansen told me, "I wouldn't be surprised if it were up to 100 additives or more that people are taking in on a daily basis."

Artificial Ingredients Are Everywhere

And it's not just food. A number of additional toxins also enter our systems from other industrial sources and often come in the form of phthalate plasticizers and parabens—both of which are used in personal care products, some medications, and even foods and food preservation. Most Americans use some form of shampoo, soap,

Many Artificial Ingredients Have Been Banned

After being in use for many years, some food additives have been found to pose serious health risks, and thus banned.

Additive	Function	Natural or Synthetic	Year Banned	Problem
Agene (nitrogen trichloride)	Flour bleaching and aging agent	Synthetic	1949	Dogs that ate bread made from treated flour suffered epileptic-like fits; the toxic agent was methionine sulfoxime.
Artificial colorings:				
Butter yellow	Artificial coloring	Synthetic	1919	Toxic, later found to cause liver cancer.
Green 1	Artificial coloring	Synthetic	1965	Liver cancer.
Green 2	Artificial coloring	Synthetic	1965	Insufficient economic importance to be tested.
Orange 1	Artificial coloring	Synthetic	1956	Organ damage.
Orange 2	Artificial coloring	Synthetic	1960	Organ damage.
Orange B	Artificial coloring	Synthetic	1978 (ban never finalized)	Contained low levels of a cancer-causing contaminant. Orange B was used only in sausage casings to color sausages, but is no longer used in the United States.
Red 1	Artificial coloring	Synthetic	1961	Liver cancer.
Red 2	Artificial coloring	Synthetic	1976	Possible carcinogen.
Red 4	Artificial coloring	Synthetic	1976	High levels damaged adrenal cortex of dog; after 1965 it was used only in maraschino cherries and certain pills; it is still allowed in externally applied drugs and cosmetics.
Red 32	Artificial coloring	Synthetic	1956	Damages internal organs and may be a weak carcinogen; since 1956 it continues to be used under the name Citrus Red 2 only to color oranges (2 ppm).
Sudan 1	Artificial coloring	Synthetic	1919	Toxic, later found to be carcinogenic.
Violet 1	Artificial coloring	Synthetic	1973	Cancer (it had been used to stamp the Department of Agriculture's inspection mark on beef.
Yellow 1 & 2	Artificial coloring	Synthetic	1959	Intestinal lesions at high dosages.
Yellow 3	Artificial coloring	Synthetic	1959	Heart damage at high dosages.
Yellow 4	Artificial coloring	Synthetic	1959	Heart damage at high dosages.
Cinnamyl Anthranilate	Artificial coloring	Synthetic	1982	Liver cancer.
Cobalt salts	Stabilize beer foam	Synthetic	1966	Toxic effects on heart.
Coumarin	Flavoring	Tonka bean	1970	Liver poison.
Cyclamate	Artificial sweetener	Synthetic	1969	Bladder cancer, damage to testes; now not thought to cause cancer directly, but to increase the potency of other carcinogens.
Diethyl Pyrocarbonate (DEPC)	Preservative (beverages)	Synthetic	1972	Combines with ammonia to form urethane, a carcinogen.
Dulcin (p-ethoxy-phenylurea)	Artificial sweetener	Synthetic	1950	Liver cancer.
Ethylene glycol	Solvent	Synthetic	1998	Kidney damage.
Monochloracetic acid	Preservative	Synthetic	1941	Highly toxic.
Nordihydroguaiaretic acid	Preservative	Desert plant	1968 (FDA) 1971 (USDA)	Kidney damage.
Oil of calamus	Flavoring	Root of Calamus	1968	Intestinal cancer.
Polyoxyethylene-8-Stearate (Myrj 45)	Emulsifier	Synthetic	1952	High levels caused bladder stones and tumors.
Safrole	Flavoring (root beer)	Sassafras	1960	Liver cancer.
Thiourea	Preservative	Synthetic	c. 1950	Liver cancer.

Taken from: Center for Science In the Public Interest, 2012.

lotion, and antiperspirant every day, and these toxins, applied to the skin, are absorbed dermally.

According to a 2010 study, like BPA, parabens and phthalates can clear our bodies relatively quickly but only if we aren't exposed to them on a regular basis. The study states, "For serious health problems to arise, exposure to these rapidly-clearing compounds must occur on a daily basis." Phthalates are associated with infertility, obesity, asthma, and allergies, as well as breast cancer; parabens are a cause for concern regarding breast cancer.

So what if it's not the dyes alone, the preservatives alone, or the BPA alone, but some haphazard combination thereof that has yet to be studied or evaluated properly? Jason August, with the FDA's Office of Food Additive Safety, admitted as much in his defense of food dyes in relation to ADHD recently when he said, "There were other factors in most of these studies that could have been the reason or could have gone hand in hand with the dyes to create these problems in these particular children, including preservatives."

This is precisely why the FDA needs to be more rigorous with its testing of individual additives and start evaluating the combined effects or "other factors" that August so blithely refers to here.

The Government Needs to Do Its Job

Chemicals used in all of these industrial products are big business—food corporations own some of the largest personal care companies and they're profiting on multiple fronts with cheap, industrial ingredients. For example, Nestlé owns 30 percent of the world's largest cosmetic and beauty company L'Oreal—tightly regulating these substances and evaluating potential harm would be a financial hardship for these corporations.

But the real hardship is placed on the American people who trust that the foods they eat are properly regulated by the government and safe for themselves and their families. How long will the FDA continue to put the health of the American people at risk with its antiquated policy? Let's hope with pressure from groups like the AAP, changing consumer demand, and continued headlines, the FDA will finally do its job.

TWO

Consumers Exaggerate the Health Threat from Artificial Ingredients

Harriet Hall

The threat from many artificial ingredients is exaggerated argues Harriet Hall in the following viewpoint. She discusses the artificial sweetener aspartame, saying that for the vast majority of people it poses no health threat, and can even have health benefits. She debunks slanderous claims made about aspartame, saying most negative publicity is either urban legend or the result of bad science. In Hall's opinion, health crusaders have used scare tactics to frighten consumers away from products that in reality pose them no harm. Other artificial ingredients, such as high fructose corn syrup, have been similarly demonized, according to Hall, who says their consumption can help overweight and obese people lose weight. She concludes that many artificial ingredients pose no health threat and are safe for the vast majority of people to consume.

Hall is a retired family physician and former US Air Force flight surgeon. An editor and one of the founding doctors of the blog *Science-Based Medicine*, Hall writes often about medicine, alternative medicine, science, and critical thinking.

Aspartame is a low calorie sugar substitute marketed under brand names like Equal and Nutrasweet. It is a combination of two amino acids: L-aspartic acid and L-phenylalanine. It is available as individual packets for adding to foods and it is a component of many diet soft drinks and other reduced-calorie foods. Depending on who you listen to, it is either a safe aid to weight loss and diabetes control or it is evil incarnate, a deadly poison that is devastating the health of consumers.

False Claims Abound

A reader sent me an ad from his local newspaper that recommended using stevia instead of aspartame and made these startling claims about aspartame:

1. It is derived from the excrement of genetically modified *E. coli* bacteria
2. Upon ingestion, it breaks down into aspartic acid, phenylalanine, methanol, formaldehyde, and formic acid.
3. It accounts for over 75% of the adverse reactions to food additives reported to the FDA [Food and Drug Administration] each year including seizures, migraines, dizzinesss, nausea, muscle spasms, weight gain, depression, fatigue, irritability, heart palpitations, breathing difficulties, anxiety, tinnitus, schizophrenia and death.

Let's look at those claims one by one.

1. In some markets, aspartame manufacture takes advantage of modern genetic laboratory processes. A plasmid introduces genes into *E. coli* bacteria; the genes are incorporated into the bacterial DNA and they increase production of enzymes that enhance the production of phenylalanine. The bacteria produce more phenylalanine, serving as little living factories. The phenylalanine these workhorses produce for us is exactly the same as phenylalanine from any other source. It is disingenuous and inflammatory to characterize it as "derived from excrement." Genetic processes like this are widely used today. One stunning example is Humulin. Diabetics used to develop allergic reactions to the beef and pork antigens in insulin derived from cows and pigs because it was

slightly different from human insulin and contained impurities. Scientists found a way to put human insulin genes into *E. coli* bacteria and put them to work producing true, pure human insulin. This was such a great advantage to diabetics that animal insulins are no longer even available.

2. Some of the things we ingest are directly absorbed and utilized unchanged, like water. But most of what we ingest is metabolized. Aspartame is metabolized. It does indeed break down into aspartic acid, phenylalanine, and methanol. Aspartic acid and phenylalanine are amino acids that we need to survive. Methanol is produced in small amounts by the metabolism of many foods; it is harmless in small amounts. A cup of tomato juice produces six times as much methanol as a cup of diet soda. Methanol is completely metabolized via formaldehyde to formic acid; no formaldehyde remains. Lastly, the formic acid is broken down into water and carbon dioxide. Human studies show that formic acid is eliminated faster than it is formed after ingestion of aspartic acid. So yes, those compounds appear, but so what? We get much larger amounts of the same compounds from our food, and they don't hurt us.

3. I searched for documentation of that claim, and I couldn't find the 75% figure anywhere. What I did find was that FD&C dyes (not aspartame) are the food additives most frequently associated with adverse reactions. Anyway, a list of reported adverse reactions is meaningless by itself. People can report any symptom they noticed after using aspartame, but they can be fooled by the *post hoc ergo propter hoc* fallacy: just because a symptom occurred after ingesting aspartame, that doesn't prove aspartame caused the symptom. Controlled studies are needed to determine if the symptom occurred more often in people using aspartame than in people not using it. Many such studies have been done and have not shown a correlation of aspartame use with any of those symptoms.

Scare Tactics and False Information

So the ad amounts to scare tactics based on false and distorted information. Actually, this ad is pretty mild compared to some of the alarmist misinformation circulating on the Internet. There

Artificial Sweeteners Are Safe in Reasonable Amounts

When determining how much of an ingredient is safe to consume, the Food and Drug Administration (FDA) uses the concept of an Acceptable Daily Intake (ADI). The ADI is a conservative estimate of the amount of sweetener that can safely be consumed on a daily basis over a person's lifetime.

The ADI for the artificial sweetener aspartame is 50 milligrams per kilogram of a person's body weight. Adults with high-level intakes of aspartame consume about 6 percent of the ADI; children, about 10 percent.

The chart below shows the approximate number of servings of various products with aspartame that people would have to consume every day to reach the ADI.

Aspartame-containing product	Approximate number of servings per day to reach the ADI Adult (150 lb)	Approximate number of servings per day to reach the ADI Child (50 lb)
Carbonated soft drink (12 oz.)	20	6
Powdered soft drink (8 oz.)	33	11
Gelatin (12 oz.)	42	14
Tabletop sweetener (packet)	97	32

Taken from: "Aspartame." The Calorie Council, 2012. www.caloriecontrol.org/sweeteners-and-lite/sugar-substitutes/aspartame.

we are told that there is a widespread epidemic of aspartame poisoning, causing headaches, seizures, Alzheimer's, cancer, diabetes, blindness, multiple sclerosis, birth defects, even Gulf War Syndrome. We are told that "If you . . . suffer from fibromyalgia symptoms, spasms, shooting pains, numbness in your legs, cramps, vertigo, dizziness, headaches, tinnitus, joint pain, depression, anxiety attacks, slurred speech, blurred vision, or memory loss—you probably have ASPARTAME DISEASE!" We are expected to believe the lie that "When they remove brain tumors, they have found high levels of aspartame in them."

All this misinformation has been identified as a hoax, an urban legend, by various sources including Time.com, Snopes.com and About.com. Much of it hinges on a widely disseminated e-mail by a "Nancy Markle" who was accused of plagiarizing it from Betty Martini. Martini is the founder of Mission Possible World Health International, which is "committed to removing the deadly chemical aspartame from our food." She is also anti-vaccine, anti-fluoride, anti-MSG, a conspiracy theorist, and thinks she was cured of breast cancer by an herbal formula.

Her website consists of misinformation, testimonials, and hysterical rants. She implores readers: YOUR personal horror story needed NOW! She is associated with a number of others notorious for circulating unreliable information, including the infamous Joseph Mercola.

There's even a book, *Sweet Poison*, by Janet Hull, creator of the Aspartame Detox Program.

Aspartame Is Very Safe

Aspartame has been found to be safe for human consumption by the regulatory agencies of more than ninety countries worldwide, with FDA officials describing aspartame as "one of the most thoroughly tested and studied food additives the agency has ever approved" and its safety as "clear cut."

When the European Commission's Scientific Committee on Food evaluated aspartame, they found over 500 papers on aspartame published between 1988 and 2001. It has been studied in animals, in various human populations including infants, children, women, obese adults, diabetics, and lactating women. Numerous studies have ruled out any association with headaches, seizures, behavior, cognition, mood, allergic reactions, and other conditions. It has been evaluated far more extensively than any other food additive.

When new rat studies by the Ramazzini Foundation in Italy appeared to show an association with tumors, the European Food Safety Authority examined Ramazzini's raw data and found errors that made them discredit the studies. Their updated opinion based on all the data available in 2009 said there was no indication of any genotoxic or carcinogenic potential of aspartame and that there was no reason to revise their previously established ADI (Acceptable Daily Intake) for aspartame of 40 mg/kg/day. Studies have shown that actual consumption is well below that limit.

People who are absolutely convinced they get adverse effects from aspartame have been proven wrong. For instance, the *New England Journal of Medicine* published a study of people who reported having headaches repeatedly after consuming aspartame. When they knew what they were consuming, 100% of them had headaches. In a double blind crossover trial, when they didn't know what they were getting, 35% had headaches after aspartame, and 45% had headaches after placebo.

Natural Is Not Always Better

Stevia comes from a plant, and the Guaraní Indians of South America have been using it to sweeten their yerba mate for centuries. The "natural fallacy" and the "ancient wisdom fallacy" sway many consumers, but for those of us who are critical thinkers, who want to avoid logical fallacies and look at the scientific evidence, what does science tell us? Is stevia preferable to aspartame? We really don't know. Concerns have been raised about possible adverse effects such as cancer and birth defects. Stevia is banned in most European countries and in Singapore and Hong Kong because their regulatory agencies felt that there was insufficient toxicological evidence to demonstrate its safety. The US banned its import in 1991 as a food additive, but the 1994 Diet Supplement Health and Education Act (DSHEA) legalized its sale as a dietary supplement. Most of the safety concerns have been dismissed, but so have the concerns about aspartame. Arguably, the concerns about stevia are more valid than those about aspartame, because there is less evidence refuting them.

Aspartame is a zero-calorie sweetener made from two amino acids that is used in many diet soft drinks and sugar substitutes.

The plant extract is refined using ethanol, methanol, crystallization and separation technologies to separate the various glycoside molecules. The Coca-Cola Company sells it as Truvia. Pepsi sells it as PureVia. It is a product of major corporations and is prepared in a laboratory using "toxic" chemicals like methanol. For some reason that doesn't bother those who are promoting stevia as a natural product.

Demonization of Artificial Ingredients Must Stop

High fructose corn syrup (HFCS) is also being demonized. "High" fructose isn't really so high. HFCS is 55% fructose. Sucrose (table sugar) is 50% fructose and 50% glucose. Honey is 50% fructose. Apples have 57% fructose; pears have 64%. Fructose has been blamed for obesity, diabetes, heart disease and a wide variety of other illnesses, but the evidence is inconclusive. Avoiding fructose would mean avoiding all sources of fructose, not just HFCS. Avoiding fruit is probably not healthy. An International Life Sciences Institute (ILSI) Expert Panel concluded that "there is no basis for recommending increases or decreases in [fructose] use in the general food supply or in special dietary use products." HFCS is 25% sweeter than sucrose, so you can use less of it and get fewer calories. Limiting total calorie intake is healthy, and both HFCS and aspartame can contribute to that goal.

Is Aspartame Safe? Yes! For everyone except people who have the genetic disorder phenylketonuria (PKU). They must avoid aspartame because they can't process phenylalanine and accumulated high levels of phenylalanine can damage their brains. Science has adequately demonstrated that aspartame is safe for everyone else.

THREE

Artificial Sweeteners Are Safe

Susan B. Roberts

Susan B. Roberts is a professor of nutrition and psychiatry at Tufts University near Boston. She is also the author of the "I" Diet, in which dieters typically lose about thirty pounds and successfully keep it off. In the following viewpoint, Roberts argues that artificial sweeteners play an important role in helping people avoid obesity. Roberts says most authoritative studies have shown that artificial sweeteners are very safe; older, more biased studies have found health risks, but Roberts says most of these were not well conducted. She also cites studies that show artificial sweeteners can prevent weight gain and may even help people lose weight. Because artificial sweeteners do not taste as good as sugar, consuming them can retrain a person's brain to crave fewer sweets, which contributes to weight loss. Roberts concludes that if a person who wants to lose weight must choose between a diet with artificial sweeteners and weight loss or one without them and weight gain, she would counsel them to consume artificial sweeteners because the benefits from weight loss are greater than the risks from the sweeteners.

For a dieter, the ultimate terror is hearing that the supposedly innocuous food or drink you've been consuming daily for God knows how long is actually a fat-filled Trojan horse. Which might be why the scare over diet soda—triggered every few years by some study that suggests that Diet Pepsi, Coke Zero, and their kin might actually make you gain weight—understandably creates some hysteria.

Controversy over whether the "high-intensity sweeteners" found in diet soda and low-calorie goods—like aspartame, sucralose, acesulfame potassium, saccharin, and Stevia—are helpful for weight control, or even safe, warrants an unbiased look at the research.

Artificial Sweeteners Are Very Safe

First, the good news: Reviews of safety continue to indicate that these products are safe (with one possible exception that I'll get to shortly). While various older studies reported increased cancer risks and other significant health concerns, when biased study designs are excluded the evidence for detectable harm gets smaller and smaller. That doesn't mean you have to use artificial sweeteners, of course—just that from the perspective of safety and health, there's no need to feel guilty about a trip to the vending machine.

The bad news is that research on the benefits of high-intensity sweeteners for weight control is extremely conflicting. Here are two examples of studies that represent about the best out there. In one five-week study conducted in 2008, 27 rats that were provided with a saccharin-sweetened yogurt ate more total food and gained more weight than rats fed sugar-sweetened yogurt. And it wasn't because they loved the saccharin-sweetened yogurt—in fact, they tended to eat less of it, but went back to their regular chow for second helpings more often than the rats given sugar. On the other hand, a 2004 study of 24 French men and women, also for about five weeks, found that the individuals randomly assigned to include high-calorie, sugar-sweetened beverages in their diet did the most overeating—and had no better hunger control compared to a similar group allocated to consume artificially sweetened beverages.

Artificial Sweeteners Serve an Important Purpose

What to make of this? What we would all like, of course, is more research so that firm conclusions can be reached without the need to triage an inadequate number of underpowered low-budget studies. Unfortunately, it's unlikely that a flood of good research is going to appear any time soon, because funding institutes like the NIH [National Institutes of Health] tend to neglect these topics, and because manufacturers of high-intensity sweeteners don't like

"High-intensity" artificial sweeteners such as sucralose, acesulfame potassium, saccharin, and aspartame are found in diet soft drinks.

to risk money on independent research that might show their product in a bad light. And while we wait hopefully for more studies, based on my own experience doing comparative research on rats and baboons in nutrition graduate school, I'll take the results from a careful study of 24 humans over a few cages of rats (however carefully studied) any day.

I'm not taking the large "observational" studies linking diet-soda consumption to weight gain too seriously—the studies that are often behind the alarming reports about diet soda making you fat. We've seen too many instances where observational studies confuse cause and effect to such an extent that they appear to prove the opposite of what really happens. In the realm of diet beverages, is it any surprise, really, that people struggling with their weight are drinking more Diet Coke? Of course not. One thing these observational studies can never show: maybe those diet-soda drinkers would have gained more weight if they weren't drinking Diet Coke.

Artificial Sweeteners Prevent Weight Gain

Which brings us to the question of what exactly are high-intensity sweeteners good for, based on the best research so far? Extrapolating from the French study, it seems reasonable to con-clude that they may help prevent weight gain if used wisely—for example, if you use them to replace sugary sodas that contain more calories than you would otherwise drink.

In my I Diet weight-loss program, I also see that high-intensity sweeteners are of substantial help to some, if not all, people dur-ing active weight loss. When you start to lose weight but have a history of craving sweets, going cold turkey on sweet treats usually doesn't work, because cravings and temptation get in the way. In this case, replacing your favorite sugar fix with something sweet-ened with a high-intensity sweetener can stave off those cravings just well enough.

Although there are insufficient research studies available to say with certainty that high-intensity sweeteners help with weight loss as much as they appear to prevent weight gain, there is indi-rect evidence suggesting this may be the case. For example, magnetic resonance imaging studies tracking the brain's responses to sugar and intense sweeteners show that in our unconscious brain we know they are different—even while we perceive both of them as "sweet-tasting" in our conscious brain. While this might seem like bad news, I view this as positive because it means we can still enjoy sweet taste without getting the neurological high that accompanies a rush of sugar calories.

A Bridge to a Healthier Lifestyle

In fact, over time, what seems plausible is that our brains can be retrained to learn that sweet taste doesn't come with calories, and we can "decondition" the synthesis of addictive chemicals like dopamine that keeps us coming back for more. In other words, using artificial sweeteners may actually make us like the real thing less over time, and provide a bridge to a healthier low-calorie, low-sugar diet that still tastes sweet due to our increased sensitivity for the sugars in natural foods.

Of course, for many people, high-intensity sweeteners don't taste the same as sugar even though they're comparably sweet. Some people notice a bitter or cold taste in diet products that contain a single sweetener (aspartame is the one commonly used alone). My suggested fix: look for products that mix them up already (for example, Coke Zero contains two sweeteners, compared to one in Diet Coke). And when sweetening something like iced tea, make your own sweetener mix by combining two or more of the common types, such as Splenda (sucralose), Equal (aspartame and acesulfame potassium), and Sweet'N Low (saccharine) or Stevia in equivalent amounts.

If that doesn't work, for drinks and other products you are sweetening yourself, try mixing artificial sweeteners with 5 or 10 percent sugar. The name of the game is fooling your brain into thinking that sweet taste is close to the real thing even when it's not.

When in Doubt Choose Artificial Sweeteners

One significant qualification to my generally positive feelings about high-intensity sweeteners: In one admittedly older study

Americans Need Help Recognizing Artificial Ingredients

A January 2010 Harris poll found that although the majority of parents with children under eighteen say they would like to avoid artificial ingredients, few are able to recognize common artificial sweeteners used in everyday foods and beverages.

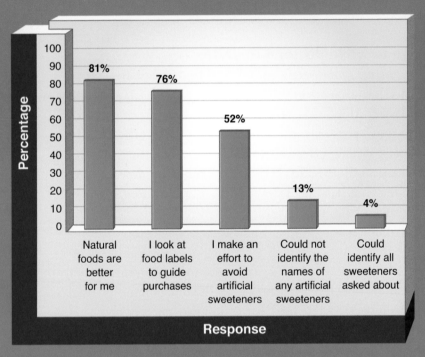

Taken from: Harris Interactive, January 2010.

of an aspartame-based product given to people suffering from depression, worsening mood was enough of a concern that the institutional review board overseeing the study stopped patient entry after only 13 subjects. That's a big thing to happen in a research study—I have never heard of such a thing happening to anyone I know, and my institute is famous for its stringent over-view process. To be sure, it's only one study, and I would love to see it repeated, but in the meantime I'm mentioning the results to my dieters so that they can make an informed choice. Fortunately, different high-intensity sweeteners have different chemical structures and metabolic effects, so even if you are concerned that one of them affects your mental state, there is no reason to assume the same will be true of another.

I wholeheartedly endorse a natural low-sugar diet without high-intensity sweeteners. But as I tell my dieters, if the choice is between weight loss with sweeteners versus no weight loss without them, I'll encourage the sweeteners any day.

FOUR

Artificial Sweeteners Are Very Dangerous

Joseph Mercola

In the following viewpoint, Joseph Mercola explains that artificial sweeteners are very dangerous to people's health. Mercola explains that the Food and Drug Administration did not approve aspartame because it was healthy or safe; rather, strong financial and political pressure led to its approval. Mercola says the government's job is to protect people from dangerous substances, not to cow to industry demands. Aspartame and other artificial sweeteners have been linked to numerous diseases, cancer, birth defects, learning disorders, and other problems, he warns. Although using some artificial sweeteners can help people lose weight, Mercola thinks their negative effects far outweigh this one positive effect. He concludes that artificial sweeteners are too toxic for human consumption and should not be available on the market.

Mercola is the author of *The No-Grain Diet* and *The Great Bird Flu Hoax* and coauthor of *Sweet Deception*. He is also the founder and editor of the website Mercola.com, which offers health articles and sells wellness products.

Aspartame is the most controversial food additive in history, and its approval for use in food was the most contested in FDA [Food and Drug Administration] history. In the end, the artificial sweetener was approved, not on scientific grounds, but rather because of strong political and financial pressure. After all, aspartame was previously listed by the Pentagon as a biochemical warfare agent!

It's hard to believe such a chemical would be allowed into the food supply, but it was, and it has been wreaking silent havoc with people's health for the past 30 years. The truth is, it should never have been released onto the market, and allowing it to remain in the food chain is seriously hurting people—no matter how many times you rebrand it under fancy new names.

The Deceptive Marketing of Aspartame

Sold commercially under names like NutraSweet, Canderel and now AminoSweet, aspartame can be found in more than 6,000 foods, including soft drinks, chewing gum, table-top sweeteners, diet and diabetic foods, breakfast cereals, jams, sweets, vitamins, prescription and over-the-counter drugs.

Aspartame producer Ajinomoto chose to rebrand it under the name AminoSweet, to "remind the industry that aspartame tastes just like sugar, and that it's made from amino acids— the building blocks of protein that are abundant in our diet."

This is deception at its finest: begin with a shred of truth, and then spin it to fit your own agenda. In this case, the agenda is to make you believe that aspartame is somehow a harmless, natural sweetener made with two amino acids that are essential for health and present in your diet already. They want you to believe aspartame delivers all the benefits of sugar and none of its drawbacks. But nothing could be further from the truth.

How Aspartame Wreaks Havoc on Your Health

Did you know there have been more reports to the FDA for aspartame reactions than for all other food additives combined? In fact, there are over 10,000 official complaints, but by the FDA's own admission, less than 1 percent of those who experience a reaction to a product ever report it. So in all likelihood, the toxic effects of aspartame may have affected roughly a million people already.

While a variety of symptoms have been reported, almost two-thirds of them fall into the neurological and behavioral category consisting mostly of headaches, mood alterations, and hallucinations. The remaining third is mostly gastrointestinal symptoms. This list will familiarize you with some of the terrifying side-effects and health problems you could encounter if you consume products containing this chemical. Unfortunately, aspartame toxicity is not well-known by doctors, despite its frequency. Diagnosis is also hampered by the fact that it mimics several other common health conditions, such as:

Multiple sclerosis,
Parkinson's disease,
Alzheimer's disease,
Fibromyalgia,
Arthritis,
Multiple chemical sensitivity,
Chronic fatigue syndrome,
Attention deficit disorder,
Panic disorder,
Depression and other psychological disorders,
Lupus [erythematosus],
Diabetes and diabetic complications,
Birth defects,
Lymphoma,
Lyme disease, and
Hypothyroidism.

How Diet Foods and Drinks CAUSE Weight Problems

In recent years, food manufacturers have increasingly focused on developing low-calorie foods and drinks to help you maintain a healthy weight and avoid obesity. Unfortunately, the science behind these products is so flawed most of these products can

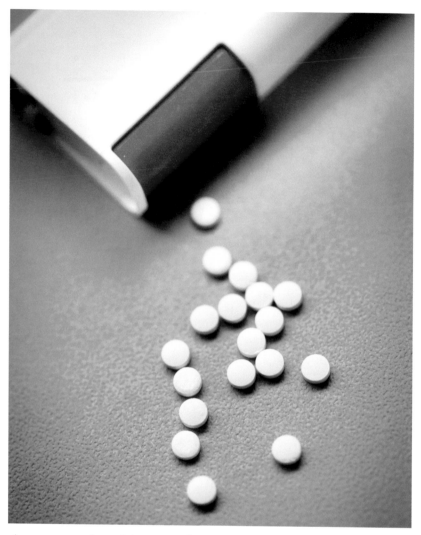

Aspartame, found in more than six thousand foods, is the most controversial food additive in history. The Food and Drug Administration admits to receiving more than ten thousand official complaints of the sweetener's toxic effects on humans.

actually lead to increased weight gain! For example, researchers have discovered that drinking diet soda increases your risk of metabolic syndrome, and may double your risk of obesity—the complete opposite of the stated intention behind these "zero calorie" drinks. The sad truth is that diet foods and drinks ruin

"To tell you the truth, I don't think the average consumer will notice, Run with it," cartoon by Marty Bucella. www.CartoonStock.com

your body's ability to count calories, and in fact stimulate your appetite, thus boosting your inclination to overindulge.

Unfortunately, most public health agencies and nutritionists in the United States recommend these toxic artificial sweeteners as an acceptable alternative to sugar, which is at best confusing and at worst harming the health of those who take their misguided advice.

Even More Toxic Dangers of Aspartame

Truly, there is enough evidence showing the dangers of consuming artificial sweeteners to fill an entire book—which is exactly why I wrote *Sweet Deception*. If you or your loved ones drink diet beverages or eat diet foods, this book will explain how you've been deceived about the truth behind artificial sweeteners like aspartame and sucralose—for greed, for profits, and at the expense of your health.

As mentioned earlier, almost two-thirds of all documented side effects of aspartame consumption are neurological.

One of the reasons for this side effect, researchers have discovered, is because the phenylalanine in aspartame dissociates from the ester bond. While these amino acids are indeed completely natural and safe, they were never designed to be ingested as isolated amino acids in massive quantities, which in and of itself will cause complications.

Additionally this will also increase dopamine levels in your brain. This can lead to symptoms of depression because it distorts your serotonin/dopamine balance. It can also lead to migraine headaches and brain tumors through a similar mechanism.

The aspartic acid in aspartame is a well-documented excitotoxin. Excitotoxins are usually amino acids, such as glutamate and aspartate. These special amino acids cause particular brain cells to become excessively excited, to the point that they die. Excitotoxins can also cause a loss of brain synapses and connecting fibers. A review conducted in 2008 by scientists from the University of Pretoria and the University of Limpopo found that consuming a lot of aspartame may inhibit the ability of enzymes in your brain to function normally, and may lead to neurodegeneration.

According to the researchers, consuming a lot of aspartame can disturb:

- The metabolism of amino acids
- Protein structure and metabolism
- The integrity of nucleic acids
- Neuronal function
- Endocrine balances

Furthermore, the ester bond in aspartame breaks down to formaldehyde and methanol, which are also toxic in their own right.

So it is not surprising that this popular artificial sweetener has also been found to cause cancer.

One truly compelling case study that shows this all too well was done by a private citizen named Victoria Inness-Brown. She decided to perform her own aspartame experiment on 108 rats over a period of 2 years and 8 months.

Daily, she fed some of the rats the equivalent (for their body weight) of two-thirds the aspartame contained in 8-oz of diet soda. Thirty-seven percent of the females fed aspartame developed tumors, some of massive size.

More Harm than Good

If you suffer from sweet cravings, it's easy to convince yourself you're doing the right thing by opting for a zero-calorie sweetener like aspartame. Please understand that you will do more harm than good to your body this way.

First, it's important to realize that your body craves sweets when you're not giving it the proper fuel it needs. Finding out your nutritional type will tell you exactly which foods you need to eat to feel full and satisfied. It may sound hard to believe right now, but once you start eating right for your nutritional type, your sweet cravings will significantly lessen and may even disappear.

Meanwhile, be sure you address the emotional component to your food cravings using a tool such as the Meridian Tapping Technique (MTT). More than any traditional or alternative method I have used or researched, MTT works to overcome food cravings and helps you reach dietary success.

And, if diet soda is the culprit for you, be sure to check out Turbo Tapping, which is an extremely effective and simple tool to get rid of your soda addiction in a short period of time.

Unacceptable Alternative Sweeteners

I have written a few articles on fructose earlier this year [2010], and I will be writing many more, so please be aware that I am

Alternatives to Artificial Ingredients

Concerns over whether artificial colorings contribute to behavioral and learning disorders such as autism or attention deficit disorder (ADD) have led some manufacturers to use natural food coloring alternatives in their products.

Artificial Coloring	Natural Food Coloring Alternative
Blue no. 1	Red cabbage
Yellow no. 5	Turmeric or saffron
Red no. 40	Beet juice
Green no. 3	Spinach extract
Orange B	Beta-carotene or paprika
Citrus Red no. 2	Purple sweet potato extract

Compiled by the editor.

absolutely convinced that fructose ingestion is at the core of our obesity epidemic.

And I'm not only talking about high fructose corn syrup, which is virtually identical to table sugar. The only major difference between the two is HFCS is much cheaper so it has contributed to massive increase in fructose ingestion, far beyond safe or healthy. Please, understand you need to keep your fructose levels BELOW 25 grams per day. The best way to do that is to avoid these "natural" sweeteners as they are loaded with a much higher percentage of fructose than HFCS.

- Fruit Juice
- Agave
- Honey

Please note that avoiding these beyond 25 grams per day is crucial, even if the source is fresh, raw, and organic. It just doesn't matter, fructose is fructose is fructose. . . .

Acceptable Alternative Sweeteners

For those times when you just want a taste of something sweet, your healthiest alternative is Stevia. It's a natural plant and, unlike aspartame and other artificial sweeteners that have been cited for dangerous toxicities, it is a safe, natural alternative that's ideal if you're watching your weight, or if you're maintaining your health by avoiding sugar. It is hundreds of times sweeter than sugar and truly has virtually no calories.

I must tell you that I am biased; I prefer Stevia as my sweetener of choice, and I frequently use it. However, like most choices, especially sweeteners, I recommend using Stevia in moderation, just like sugar. In excess it is still far less likely to cause metabolic problems than sugar or any of the artificial sweeteners.

I want to emphasize, that if you have insulin issues, I suggest that you avoid sweeteners altogether, including Stevia, as they all can decrease your sensitivity to insulin.

Lo han is another sweetener like Stevia. It's an African sweet herb that can also be used, but it's a bit more expensive and harder to find.

So if you struggle with high blood pressure, high cholesterol, diabetes or extra weight, then you have insulin sensitivity issues and would benefit from avoiding ALL sweeteners. But for everyone else, if you are going to sweeten your foods and beverages anyway, I strongly encourage you to consider using regular Stevia or Lo han, and toss out all artificial sweeteners and any products that contain them.

FIVE

It Is Difficult to Determine the Safety of Artificial Ingredients

Marion Nestle, as told to the *San Francisco Chronicle*

Marion Nestle is a professor of nutrition and public policy at New York University. In the following viewpoint taken from an interview with the *San Francisco Chronicle* newspaper, she discusses why it is difficult to prove whether artificial ingredients are safe or harmful. Artificial ingredients, pesticides, and other chemicals are present in foods in very tiny amounts, and it is difficult to prove their harm or safety at such minuscule levels. Nestle explains that when there is not enough evidence to be sure of an ingredient's safety, it can be approached in one of two ways: either ban the substance until it can be proven safe, or keep it legal until it can be proven harmful. Companies that sell products with such substances prefer the latter approach, claiming it is not fair to prohibit their sale without direct scientific evidence that proves them harmful. Nestle says concerned consumers must take matters into their own hands and avoid substances they have reason to believe are probably unsafe, even if the government is unwilling to ban them without hard evidence.

San Francisco Chronicle: I don't understand why the FDA does not ban aspartame, food colors, BPA [bisphenol A], pesticides and all those other nasty chemicals in food. I can't believe they are good for us.

Marion Nestle: I can't, either. But the Food and Drug Administration [FDA] is required to make decisions on the basis of science, not beliefs. You eat these chemicals in tiny amounts—parts per billion or trillion. Whether doses this low cause harm is hard to assess for two reasons: science and politics. Scientists cannot easily measure the health effects of exposure to low-dose chemicals. And the industries that make and use these chemicals don't want to give them up.

The Problem of Low Doses

Food chemicals elicit plenty of public dread and outrage. But are they harmful? Controlled clinical trials at normal levels of intake would require vast numbers of subjects over decades. Nobody would fund them. Instead, researchers use animals consuming much higher doses. I can remember how the diet soda industry ridiculed studies suggesting that saccharine caused bladder cancer in rats: the doses were equivalent to drinking 1,250 12-ounce diet sodas a day.

The difficulties of doing research on low-dose chemicals—and the food industry's insistence that such doses are safe—explains the FDA's reluctance to act. Some examples illustrate the problem.

Some studies suggest that aspartame might cause cancer in rats when consumed at levels typical of diet soft drinks, as well as other problems. But researchers performing better controlled studies have given aspartame a clean bill of health. Despite public concerns, the FDA's assessment of the evidence "finds no reason to alter its previous conclusion that aspartame is safe as a general purpose sweetener in food."

Not Enough Evidence to Conclude

[Food dyes] have been considered a possible cause of hyperactivity in children since the 1970s. Some studies show improved behavior among children placed on additive-free diets. But behavior

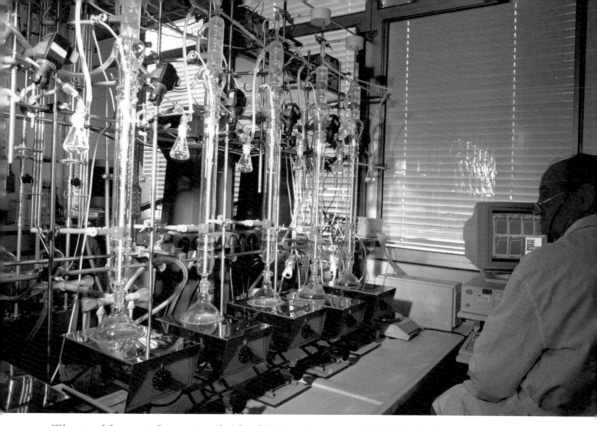

The problem with testing food additives in controlled clinical trials is that assessing normal intake levels takes a vast number of subjects monitored over decades. Researchers instead use animals that consume the additives in much higher doses in a shorter time span.

is difficult to judge objectively, and even controlled studies gave mixed results.

A recent study funded by the British Food Standards Agency is typical. It found most children to be unaffected by removing additives. But a small percentage seemed to get better. The FDA can only conclude that there is not enough science to decide whether food dyes cause hyperactivity.

Two Ways to Approach the Problem

BPA (bisphenol a) is a component of hard plastic used to make baby bottles and food and beverage cans. It is also an endocrine

The Lucrative Food Additive Market

Critics of efforts to ban artificial ingredients say the food additive market is a lucrative industry that generates billions of dollars each year. Banning such ingredients would cripple vital sectors in all of the world's regional economies.

Global Sales of Food Additives ($m)

Region	2005	2008	2010
North America	7,116.67	7,962.35	8,598.51
Europe	8,198.37	9,183.57	10,015.53
Asia	5,196.72	6,006.73	6,673.80
Rest of world	3,158.03	3,579.20	3,927.64
Total	23,719.79	26,731.85	29,215.48

Taken from: Global Industry Analysts. "How Banning Artificial Food Additives Would Impact Chemical Industry." ICIS, April 24, 2008. www.icis.com/Articles/2008/04/28/9118968/how-banning-artificial-food-additives-would -impact-chemical-industry.html.

disrupter. Last year [2010], the FDA concluded that BPA is safe at current exposure levels. At the same time, the FDA advised children and pregnant women to reduce exposure to BPA. It advised the infant formula and soda industries to find ways to replace it. The California Legislature has passed AB1319 banning BPA from baby bottles and sippy cups; it's awaiting Gov. Jerry Brown's signature. [*Editor's note: Gov. Brown signed AB 1319 into law several days after this interview was published.*]

Recent studies raise concerns about BPA's effects on the brain and behavior of fetuses, infants and young children, and on cancer, obesity and infertility in adults. Some studies suggest that exposure to BPA is higher than previously estimated. Just last week, the Breast Cancer Fund released a study finding BPA in canned foods designed for children.

Studies by university scientists tend to find harm from BPA at low doses, whereas those by government regulatory agencies and the food industry do not. In the absence of compelling science, regulators have two choices: exercise the "precautionary principle" and ban the chemical until it can be proven safe, or approve it until it can be shown to be harmful. The United States and European safety agencies—and the food industry, of course— prefer the latter approach.

Research clearly demonstrates that pesticides harm farmworkers exposed to high doses. But recent studies report slightly lower IQ levels in children born to urban women with higher blood levels of pesticides. Although these studies did not control for socioeconomic and other variables that might influence IQ, they raise the possibility that even low levels might be harmful.

Take Personal Action

While waiting for the science to evolve, you can take both personal and political action. You don't want potentially harmful chemicals in your foods? Read labels and don't buy foods with artificial sweeteners or food colors. Kids don't need them anyway. Consumer action has already induced baby bottle makers to get rid of BPA. This strategy can work for food colors, too.

Don't stop eating fruits and vegetables. Their known health benefits greatly outweigh the potential harm of pesticides. Don't stop eating them. Buy organic. Pesticides, invisible and unlabeled as they are, constitute a good reason to do so.

Get political. Let your congressional representatives know that more research is needed, but you don't want to wait for it. You want industry to find healthier alternatives.

SIX

Artificial Ingredients Cause Behavioral Problems in Children

David W. Schab and Michael F. Jacobson

In the following viewpoint David W. Schab and Michael F. Jacobson argue that food dyes cause learning disorders and behavioral problems in children. They explain that foods are artificially colored because dye is a cheap, shelf-stable way to make foods seem more fun, delicious, or otherwise alluring. But in reality, warn Schab and Jacobson, such dyes contribute to hyperactivity, attention deficit disorder, and other developmental problems in children. The authors explain that chemical companies and food distributors have historically enjoyed a powerful influence over government regulators. As a result, say the authors, the US government has been less strict than other countries about the use of artificial ingredients. Schab and Jacobson conclude that food can be attractive, appetizing, and delicious without the use of harmful food dyes and that Americans deserve a government that will protect them from eating harmful substances.

Schab is an assistant clinical professor of psychiatry at Columbia University. Jacobson is the executive director of the Center for Science in the Public Interest, a consumer advocacy group.

Today's supermarket is a fun house of hues. Its aisles feature riotously colored processed foods perfectly engineered to appeal to the part of your brain that says "yum": Technicolor Starburst candy. Polychromatic Froot Loops. A rainbow of flavored juices.

Those hyper-saturated colors have come to seem normal, even natural, like the come-ons of tropical fruits. But they are increasingly produced through the magic of artificial food dyes, applied not just to candies and snack foods but to such seemingly all-natural products as pickles, salad dressing and some oranges.

Dyes Endanger Children

Artificial dyes aren't just making your Yoplait Light Red Raspberry yogurt blush and your Kraft Macaroni and Cheese glow in the dark. They are causing behavioral problems and disrupting children's attention, according to a growing number of scientific studies. On [March 23, 2011], following the lead of European regulators, a Food and Drug Administration [FDA] advisory committee will begin a review of research on the behavioral effects of artificial dyes. In a significant turn from the agency's previous denials that dyes have any influence on children's behavior, an FDA staff report released [in early March 2011] concluded that synthetic food colorings do affect some children.

The agency should take action. Allowing the use of artificial dyes violates the FDA's mandate to protect consumers from unsafe products. It also runs afoul of the agency's mandate to crack down on food that has been made "to appear better or of greater value than it is."

Centuries of Concern About Artificial Ingredients

Concern about food dye is long-standing. In the 1800s, American food manufacturers began doctoring their wares with toxic pigments made from lead and copper. In the second half of that century, a revolution in organic chemistry brought artificial dyes made from coal tar—a relative advance over lead.

At the turn of the 20th century, margarine producers were making the most of the technology: They added new yellow dyes to their colorless product to better compete with butter. But the dairy industry lobbied for bans and taxes on colored margarine, and state legislatures and Congress obliged. Consumers who wanted their margarine yellow could open a separate packet of dye and mix it in themselves.

In 1906, Congress took up the question of whether artificial dyes were bad for consumers, with the first of several major acts. The most recent and stringent of them, passed in 1960, banned color additives that caused cancer in humans or animals. But the fate of one such additive, Red 3, illustrates how even strong legislation can be thwarted. Lab rats that were fed large amounts of the dye developed thyroid cancer, so in 1984 the acting FDA commissioner recommended banning it. However, fruit-cocktail producers, who relied on the dye to brighten maraschino cherries, pleaded with the Department of Agriculture to block the move. As a result, the FDA banned Red 3 only in cosmetics and topical drugs.

In the early 1990s, FDA and Canadian scientists found that Red 40, Yellow 5 and Yellow 6, the three most widely used dyes, were contaminated with likely human carcinogens. And while many foods, such as M&M's and Kellogg's Hot Fudge Sundae Pop Tarts, include as many as five different dyes, even today the carcinogenic potential of such combinations has not been tested.

Despite those concerns, parents continued to serve up meals and stuff their children's lunchboxes with more and more processed foods colored with dyes, stoking a five-fold increase in the per-capita production of food dyes over the past 50 years.

An Increase in Learning and Behavioral Problems

Over the same period, psychiatrists and teachers were seeing more attention and behavioral problems, while allergists were raising concerns about Yellow 5. Physician Benjamin Feingold's 1975 book, "Why Your Child Is Hyperactive," along with the additive-free diet it promoted, spawned numerous studies on the effect of additives on attention-deficit disorders.

These jelly beans contain artificial dyes. In a study in 2004 the author found evidence that hyperactive children who consumed such dyes became significantly more hyperactive than those who received a placebo.

In 2004, one of us co-authored an analysis of the best studies of food dyes' effects on behavior. That analysis found striking evidence that hyperactive children who consumed dyes became significantly more hyperactive than children who got a placebo.

At the same time, the British government funded two studies, each involving almost 300 children. Their results were even more startling: Artificial food dyes (in combination with a common preservative) could make even children with no known behavioral problems hyperactive and inattentive.

Health officials in the United Kingdom urged manufacturers to stop using the six dyes—including Red 40, Yellow 5 and Yellow 6—involved in those studies. Next, the European Parliament required that foods containing those chemicals bear a label warning that the dyes "may have an adverse effect on activity and attention in children." That is seen by some as the death knell for artificial dyes throughout Europe.

High Color, Low Nutrient

Beyond the behavioral problems and cancer risks, the greatest hazard that dyes pose for children may also be the most obvious: They draw kids away from nutritious foods and toward brightly colored processed products that are high in calories but low in nutrients, such as fruit-flavored drinks and snack foods. Those types of foods are a major force in America's obesity epidemic, which, according to the Society of Actuaries [an insurance industry organization], costs the nation $270 billion a year.

Artificial colorings are explicitly meant to manipulate consumers' perceptions. Manufacturers tout research showing that redness enhances the impression of sweetness, and that in tests with beverages and sherbets, the color of the product did more to influence consumers' perception of the flavor than the flavor itself. One dye marketer states that its colorings offer "a limitless palette, unmatched technology and the emotional connection between people and color."

An Undyed World Can Still Be Appetizing

A world without harmful dyes does not mean a future of blandly beige snacks. A range of vivid natural colorings, made largely from plant extracts, is already in use in Europe and to a lesser extent in the United States. In Britain, for example, McDonald's Strawberry Sundaes are made without artificial coloring; here, Red 40 adds to the strawberry color. Both the British and American formulations of Nutri-Grain Strawberry cereal bars contain strawberries, but in Britain plant-based colorings add extra color, while in the United States Red 40 does the job.

Fortunately, some U.S. companies are switching to colorings found in nature. The bountiful shelves of Whole Foods and Trader Joe's are devoid of dyes, Necco has dropped artificial dyes from its iconic wafers [but later again started using them], and

Starbucks has banned dyes from its baked goods and drinks. Most companies will resist, because artificial dyes are brighter, cheaper and more stable than natural colorings. It's also a nuisance for them to reformulate their dyed products—and the government has given them no incentive to change.

Today, Britons enjoy all the colorful foods they have come to expect without many of the health risks they learned to avoid. Here, we get the same foods—but until the FDA bans synthetic dyes, we get them with a side order of dangerous and unnecessary chemicals.

SEVEN

The Link Between Artificial Ingredients and Behavioral Problems Is Unproven

Rob Johnston

Artificial ingredients do not necessarily cause behavioral problems in children, argues Rob Johnston in the following viewpoint. He contends that the link between artificial ingredients and behavioral problems is unproven at best and completely wrong at worst. He claims that bans on artificial ingredients are based on studies that used faulty science and were not universally endorsed. He accuses the British government of banning substances not out of belief that they are truly harmful but out of a desire to appear as if they are doing something good for the public. Johnston thinks it is wrong to ban artificial ingredients if there is only weak or disputed evidence linking them to behavioral problems. In his opinion, panic over artificial ingredients causes more damage than the ingredients themselves.

Johnston writes about environmental, health, and science issues for *Spiked*, an online alternative publication.

Whether food additives have any negative effect on children is open to question, yet the board of the UK Food Standards Agency (FSA) definitely seems to be suffering from hyperactivity. Last Thursday [April 10, 2008], the FSA asked UK food and drink manufacturers to stop using six colouring agents by the end of the 2008, even though the study used to justify this demand was seriously criticised by the FSA's counterparts in Europe.

Additives also seem to cause agitation at the University of Southampton, which produced the latest inconclusive research and is pitching for an extra £5.25 million grant to do the work properly. Professor Jim Stevenson, leader of the Southampton team, stoked up pressure on the FSA by suggesting that additives could be as 'dangerous as lead in petrol' [gasoline], a type of 'campaigning science' reminiscent of Dr Andrew Wakefield and the MMR scare.[1]

This latest pronouncement from the FSA follows a course tried and tested by this government:

1. Commission a study—then ignore the results;
2. Ask 'experts' to review the study—then ignore their recommendations;
3. Do what the most hysterical sections of the media want you to;
4. Pretend to have acted decisively—and 'in the public interest'.

Overly Strict Policy Based on Bad Science

The Southampton study was published in the *Lancet* in 2007. It aimed to detect 'hyperactivity' when children were given one of two different mixtures of four artificial colourings (from the six 'suspects') plus the 'natural' preservative sodium benzoate.

There are a number of problems with the Southampton study. For example, food scarists have been campaigning against sodium

---

1. Wakefield was the lead author of a 1998 British study claiming that the measles, mumps, and rubella (MMR) vaccine caused autism in children. The study was later repudiated, and Wakefield is no longer a licensed physician.

benzoate for years because they believe it causes hyperactivity on its own. If they're right, the entire Southampton study is meaningless because *both* active mixtures contained significant amounts of sodium benzoate.

Stevenson *et al* claim that the mixtures of additives and sodium benzoate produced significantly more hyperactivity in three-year-olds and eight- to nine-year-olds than did placebo drinks.

But they could not determine which of the five ingredients in each mixture (seven in total) might be responsible.

Members of the EU [European Union] can only take unilateral action on additives 'if there is evidence of a serious risk to public health'. Because the Southampton study did not contain such evidence, in 2007 the FSA said it would do nothing and passed the buck to the European Food Standards Agency (EFSA).

Officials Want to Ban Substances Without Good Evidence

The EFSA considered the Southampton study for six months. Its report, published on 14 March 2008, was damning. Among its criticisms were the following:

- The results were too confused to make any sensible conclusions. Findings were inconsistent with respect to age, gender of the children, or which of the two additive mixtures was used;
- Results were only positive using the assessment of parents but not by those of teachers, 'independent observers' or computer monitoring;
- Hyperactivity was measured with a new and unproven combination of criteria;
- Effect could have been caused by any one of the seven different individual additives;
- There was no information on whether high doses made children more hyperactive than low doses or how long after ingestion any effects occurred.

The EFSA concluded that 'the findings of the study cannot be used as a basis for altering the ADI [acceptable daily intake] of the respective food colours or sodium benzoate'.

In a strangely worded retort, Professor Stevenson admitted that 'the effects of individual additives and dose-response effects . . . were never going to be addressed by the Southampton Study' because the FSA had not provided enough funding. Stevenson said he might be able to answer the right questions with (at least) another £5.25million. Undeterred, Stevenson continued to demand a ban on all six additives; the FSA has now endorsed his view.

Food Scarists Spread False Alarm

This call can only spread unjustified alarm, particularly when FSA focus groups reveal widespread popular ignorance about what is added to food. Many members of the public believe that 'all additives are bad' and that 'the higher the E number, the worse it is' (E numbers are simply codes for food additives used in the European Union). Instead of providing better information, the FSA deliberately stoked up anxiety last year [2007] with a new website—ActionOnAdditives.com—which encourages worried parents to spot and report products that contain the 'suspect six' colouring agents. So far, over 900 such products have been identified—solely to create the impression that the FSA is 'doing something'.

The FSA has changed from a proper regulatory body to one driven by PR [public relations]. There has always been an inclination at the FSA to overreact to food scares, as illustrated by the agency's response to the discovery of Sudan I food dye in some ready meals in 2005. But the rot really seems to have started two years ago when the distinguished scientist Sir John Krebs retired as the FSA's chair and was replaced by Dame Deirdre Hutton. Hutton is a former chair of the National Consumer Council and a long-term quangocrat [one who rules according to the advice of a "quango," or quasi-autonomous non-governmental organisation] with a host of agencies renowned for knee-jerk reactions

The author criticizes the British Food Standards Agency (FSA) for ignoring its own food study results as well as outside experts' recommendations on food additives.

to media pressure—including the Sustainable Development Commission, various divisions of the Environment Agency and Energy Advisory Panels.

Officials Ignore What Is Inconvenient

Ironically, Dame Deirdre gave a major speech in Dublin [in 2007], entitled 'Why evidence is essential', which concluded: 'We need authoritative evidence. Evidence that identifies the most effective levers and tools that help people make changes for themselves. Evidence that convinces the food industry to produce and promote healthier foods. And evidence powerful enough, and thoughtfully conveyed, which helps people change eating habits that have been ingrained over a lifetime.'

When it comes to pandering to the [British tabloid the] *Daily Mail*'s campaign against 'additives', Dame Deidre and her bold new FSA demonstrate that most crucial aspect of the modern approach to 'evidence'—ignore whatever is inconvenient.

EIGHT

Artificial Food Colorings Should Be Banned

Center for Science in the Public Interest

> The Center for Science in the Public Interest (CSPI) is a nonprofit consumer watchdog group that advocates for sound nutritional, health, and food-safety policy in the United States. In the following viewpoint, it explains why artificial food colorings should be banned. Such dyes contain toxic chemicals that are not safe in the amounts in which humans currently consume them, argues the author, stating that these chemicals have been linked with cancer, behavioral, developmental, and other health problems, and are particularly dangerous to children. The CSPI suggests that it is easy and safe to use natural food colorings, such as beet juice and red cabbage. It urges governmental agencies to ban artificial food colorings that cannot be proven unequivocally safe, maintaining that the government has an obligation to protect its citizens, not the corporations that make products containing artificial food dyes.

It is said that we "eat with our eyes as much as with our mouths," and that's certainly the case when we walk down the aisles of a supermarket. Fresh produce beckons us with its vivid colors and organic shapes, brightly colored packages and images seek to draw our eyes to those brands instead of competitors, and countless products—from Jell-O to Froot Loops—are colored with bright synthetic dyes that turn unattractive mixtures of basic ingredients and food additives into alluring novelties.

An Overreliance on Dyes

Dyes are complex organic chemicals that were originally derived from coal tar, but now from petroleum. Companies like using them because they are cheaper, more stable, and brighter than most natural colorings. However, consumers' growing preference for natural foods is leading some companies to either not add colorings or to switch to safe natural colorings, such as beta-carotene (a precursor to vitamin A), paprika, beet juice, and turmeric. That trend is stronger in Europe than the United States, but some U.S. companies recognize that an "All Natural" label can attract customers and may be moving in that direction.

Unlike other food additives, dyes are not permitted to be used unless the U.S. Food and Drug Administration (FDA) has tested and certified that each batch meets the legal specifications. One benefit of the certification process is that it provides information about the amounts of dyes sent into commerce each year for use in foods, drugs, and cosmetics. Just three dyes—Red 40, Yellow 5, and Yellow 6—account for 90 percent of all dyes used. The FDA's data show a dramatic five-fold increase in consumption of dyes since 1955. That increase is a good indication of how Americans increasingly have come to rely on processed foods, such as soft drinks, breakfast cereals, candies, snack foods, baked goods, frozen desserts, and even pickles and salad dressings, that are colored with dyes.

Carcinogenicity Is Difficult to Determine

Long-term animal feeding studies are done to determine whether long-term exposure to dyes causes cancer or other effects. However, most of the studies reviewed in this report suffer from several significant limitations. First, most of the studies were commissioned or conducted by dye manufacturers, so biases could influence the design, conduct, or interpretation of the studies.

Ideally, the tests would have been conducted and interpreted by independent scientists. Second, most of the studies lasted no longer than two years—and some were much shorter. Also, many studies did not include an *in utero* [in-the-womb] phase. Chronic bioassays [long-term tests] would be more sensitive if they lasted from conception through 30 months or the natural lives of the rodents (as long as 3 years).

Another consideration of unknown importance is that virtually all the studies evaluated the safety of individual dyes. Many foods, though, contain mixtures of dyes, such as the Blue 1, Blue 2, Red 40, Yellow 5, and Yellow 6 in Kellogg's Hot Fudge Sundae Pop Tarts. Dyes conceivably could have synergistic (or, indeed, antagonistic) effects with one another or with other food additives or ingredients.

It is worth noting that dyes are not pure chemicals, but may contain upwards of 10 percent impurities that are in the chemicals from which dyes are made or develop in the manufacturing process. For instance, Yellow 5, the second-most widely used dye, may contain up to 13 percent of a witch's brew of organic and inorganic chemicals.

Certain of those contaminants, such as 4-aminobiphenyl, 4-aminoazobenzene, and benzidine, are carcinogens, but are supposed to be present at safely negligible levels in the dyes. Any carcinogenic effects of those low-level contaminants would not be detected in animal studies of the dyes.

An Error-Prone Process

The FDA has established legal limits for cancer-causing contaminants in dyes. Those limits are intended to ensure that a dye will not pose a lifetime risk of greater than one cancer in one million people. FDA chemists test each batch of dye to confirm that those tolerances are not exceeded. Unfortunately, the FDA's process is riddled with problems.

For one thing, those tolerances were based on 1990 dye usage, but per-capita usage has increased by about 50 percent since then. Second, the FDA did not consider the increased risk that dyes

Food dyes were originally developed from coal tar, but are now made more cheaply from petroleum. Dyes shown here include yellow no. 5, blue no. 1, and red no. 40.

pose to children, who are both more sensitive to carcinogens and consume more dyes per unit of body weight than adults. Third, and most importantly, FDA and Canadian government scientists showed that levels of bound benzidine, a carcinogenic contaminant in at least Yellow 5 and Yellow 6 dyes, far exceeded levels of free dyes. (Bound carcinogens have also been found in Allura Red AC, the un-certified form of Red 40). Indeed, the Canadians found several bound carcinogens in soft drinks and hard candies. Bound benzidine is largely converted to the free form in the large intestine. Large amounts of other carcinogenic contaminants might also be present in the bound form.

However, the FDA generally only measures "free" contaminants and, hence, is blind to those (except possibly aniline) bound up in other molecules. Fourth, the FDA should consider the cumulative risk of all dyes, rather than of each dye independently. Indeed, the Food, Drug, and Cosmetic Act requires the FDA to consider "the cumulative effect, if any, of such additive . . . taking into account the same or any chemically or pharmacologically related substance . . . " If the FDA considered those four factors in evaluating risks, the risks posed by the two yellow dyes—which comprise 49 percent of all dyes used—let alone all dyes taken together, would exceed the one-in-a-million standard. . . .

Food Dyes and the Law

A 1914 editorial in *The Journal of Industrial and Engineering Chemistry* stated that "America can have a coal-tar dye industry if she pays the price". Unfortunately, America did develop a coal-tar dye industry, and we may well be paying a kind of price that the journal editors did not have in mind. Down through the years, more food dyes have been found to be risky than any other category of food additive. . . .

Some Members of Congress have emphasized that the safety standard for artificial colorings should be particularly high because the colorings don't offer any health benefit to offset even small risks. Representative Ted Weiss (D-NY) said, "It doesn't make any difference how much or how little (of a carcinogenic additive) a particular substance contains, especially when you've got a color additive that has no nutrient value and no therapeutic value". Representative King said, "The colors which go into our foods and cosmetics are in no way essential to the public interest or the national security . . . Consumers will easily get along without (carcinogenic colors)".

Consumer activists have long sought to persuade the FDA to ban dyes. In the early 1970s, CSPI urged the government to ban Violet No. 1, which, ironically, was the color used in the U.S. Department of Agriculture's meat inspection stamp, because it appeared to cause cancer in animal studies (the dye was banned in 1973). Subsequently, in the 1970s and 1980s, Public Citizen's Health Research Group was the most aggressive critic of dyes, petitioning and suing the FDA to ban dyes. Some of those actions were based on the 1960 law—the Delaney amendment—that bans the use of colorings that cause cancer in animals or humans. Also, as noted above, in 2008 CSPI urged the FDA to ban colors because of their effects on children's behavior.

Even if color additives were all deemed to be safe, many uses of colorings, both synthetic and natural, still could be considered illegal under the Food, Drug, and Cosmetic Act. Sections 402(b)(3) and (b)(4) of that law stipulate that "A food shall be deemed to be adulterated . . . (3) if damage or inferiority has been concealed in any manner; or (4) if any substance has been added thereto or mixed or packed therewith so as to . . . make it appear better or of greater value than it is." And section 403 of the same law says that a food is misbranded "if its labeling is false or misleading in any particular."

Americans Want to Know What They Are Eating

Clearly, food colorings are added to fruit drinks, frozen desserts, gelatin desserts, salad dressings, child-oriented breakfast cereals and snack foods, and countless other products solely to conceal the absence of fruits, vegetables, or other ingredients and make the food "appear better or of greater value than it is." Defenders of colorings would say that consumers could simply plow through the list of ingredients on the back of the package to detect the presence of colorings, but it simply isn't fair to require consumers to do that plowing. Currently, the use of artificial flavorings must be declared conspicuously as part of the product names on the front labels. If nothing else, the FDA should require the same of artificially colored foods. A national Internet-based poll commissioned by CSPI and conducted by Opinion Research Corporation in January 2010 found that 74 percent of respondents favored such labeling.

As this report discusses, studies of the nine dyes currently approved by the FDA suggest, if not prove, that most of the dyes cause health problems, including cancer, hypersensitivity, or neurotoxicity (including hyperactivity). And that's the case even though most of the research was commissioned, conducted, and interpreted by the chemical industry itself and its testing labs and academic consultants. The health concerns indicate that most dyes fail the FDA's safety requirement "that there is convincing evidence . . . that no harm will result from the intended use of the color additive." Fortunately, numerous natural colorings could be used in place of dyes: beet juice, beta-caramel, carotene, carrot juice, chlorophyll, elderberry juice, grape juice/skin, paprika extract, purple corn, purple sweet potato, red cabbage, and turmeric.

Getting Dyes Out of Foods

CSPI has urged several major multinational companies that do not use dyes in Europe to do the same in the United States. Unfortunately, most of those companies said that they don't use dyes in Europe because government has urged them not to—but that they would continue to use dyes in the United States until they were ordered not to or consumers demanded such foods. (Starbucks and the maker of NECCO Wafers have eliminated dyes, and Frito-Lay said that it would be phasing out dyes in the coming years).

Consumers should not have to wait decades, if not forever, for companies to voluntarily remove questionable dyes from their products. The FDA, which is charged with protecting the public from unsafe food ingredients, should ban most or all of the dyes. However, it is worth noting that the Food, Drug, and Cosmetic Act makes it even harder for the FDA to revoke previous approvals of food colors than other food additives. As one legal analyst stated,

> Thanks to the foresight and effective lobbying of the cosmetics industry in the 1960s, the proponent of a color additive petition is in an excellent position if the FDA decides to remove [a coloring's] permanent listing. The burdens of proof in a complex process fall on the FDA, and the time required to pass through the procedural maze acts as a disincentive to FDA undertaking any delisting action.

Awash in Food Dyes

There has been a five-fold increase in the use and consumption of food dyes since 1955.

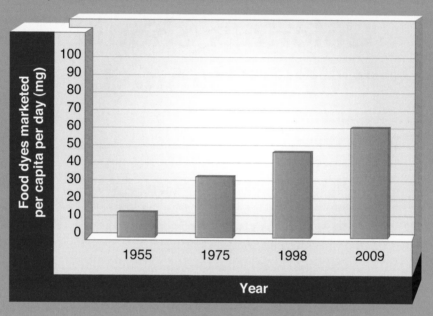

Source: *Food Dyes: A Rainbow of Risks.* Center for Science and the Public Interest, June 2010, pp. 1–2.

Ideally the law would be changed to provide greater consumer protection from unsafe dyes. . . . The time has come to eliminate dyes from our food supply and return to the use of natural colorings (or foods that don't require colorings to be marketable), the direction in which Europe—and some American companies—are moving.

NINE

Artificial Food Colorings Should Not Be Banned

Gardiner Harris

Food colorings should not be banned, argues Gardiner Harris in the following viewpoint. He explains that consumer advocacy groups like the Center for Science in the Public Interest have lobbied to get food colorings banned, saying they are a threat to public health and are only used to sell junk food to children. But Harris argues that food coloring is an important part of the eating experience. Artificial colorings give foods an appetizing look, and even trick a person's brain into thinking the food tastes good. Harris says that the government has concluded that food colorings are safe, and foods that contain them bear a label so suspicious consumers can avoid them if they want to do so. Although some advocacy groups have recommended replacing artificial food colorings with natural ones, Harris argues that these are not a good substitute. Natural colorings fade quickly, so the products they are part of have a shorter shelf life, which affects their market value. Harris concludes that artificially colored foods make eating the fun, delicious, and indulgent activity it is meant to be.

Harris is a science reporter for the *New York Times*.

Without the artificial coloring FD&C Yellow No. 6, Cheetos Crunchy Cheese Flavored Snacks would look like the shriveled larvae of a large insect. Not surprisingly, in taste tests, people derived little pleasure from eating them. Their fingers did not turn orange. And their brains did not register much cheese flavor, even though the Cheetos tasted just as they did with food coloring.

"People ranked the taste as bland and said that they weren't much fun to eat," said Brian Wansink, a professor at Cornell University and director of the university's Food and Brand Lab.

A Colorless Food World Is Unappetizing

Naked Cheetos would not seem to have much commercial future. Nor might some brands of pickles. The pickling process turns them an unappetizing gray. Dye is responsible for their robust green. Gummi worms without artificial coloring would look like, well, muddily translucent worms. Jell-O would emerge out of the refrigerator a watery tan.

No doubt the world would be a considerably duller place without artificial food coloring. But might it also be a safer place? The Center for Science in the Public Interest, an advocacy group, asked the government [in late March 2011] to ban artificial coloring

Food dyes make food more appealing; if, for example, these pickles were not dyed green, they would appear an unappetizing gray.

because the dyes that are used in some foods might worsen hyperactivity in some children.

"These dyes have no purpose whatsoever other than to sell junk food," [states] Marion Nestle, a professor of nutrition, food studies and public health at New York University.

Color Is a Part of the Eating Experience

A government advisory panel concluded that there was no proof that dyes caused problems in most children, and that whatever problems they might cause in some children did not warrant a ban or a warning label beyond what is already required—a disclosure on the product label that artificial colors are present.

"Color is such a crucial part of the eating experience that banning dyes would take much of the pleasure out of life," said Kantha Shelke, a food chemist and spokeswoman for the Institute of Food Technologists. "Would we really want to ban everything when only a small percentage of us are sensitive?" Indeed, color often defines flavor in taste tests. When tasteless yellow coloring is added to vanilla pudding, consumers say it tastes like banana or lemon pudding. And when mango or lemon flavoring is added to white pudding, most consumers say that it tastes like vanilla pudding. Color creates a psychological expectation for a certain flavor that is often impossible to dislodge, Dr. Shelke said. "Color can actually override the other parts of the eating experience," she said in an interview.

Natural Colorings Not Good Substitutes

Even so, some food companies have expanded their processed-product offerings to include foods without artificial colorings. You can now buy Kool-Aid Invisible, for instance, and Kraft Macaroni and Cheese Organic White Cheddar. Some grocery chains, including Whole Foods Market and Trader Joe's, refuse to sell foods with artificial coloring.

As yet, natural colorings have not proven to be a good alternative. They are generally not as bright, cheap or stable as artificial colorings, which can remain vibrant for years. Natural colorings often fade within days.

Food Dye Certification by the FDA in Fiscal Year 2009

The FDA has approved numerous food dyes for human consumption.

Food Dye	Pounds of Total Dye Certified	Percentage of Total
Blue 1 21 CFR 74.101	711,659	4.7
Blue 2 21 CFR 74.102	550,883	3.7
Citrus Red 2 21 CFR 74.302	1,764	0.0
Green 3 21 CFR 74.203	15,817	0.1
Orange B 21 CFR 74.250	0	0.0
Red 3 21 CFR 74.303	216,235	1.4
Red 40 21 CFR 74.340	6,205,374	41.3
Yellow 5 21 CFR 74.705	3,756,551	25.0
Yellow 6 21 CFR 74.706	3,558,351	23.7
Total	15,016,634	100

Taken from: Center for Science in the Public Interest. "Food Dyes: A Rainbow of Risks," June 2010, pp. 1–2.

Todd Miller, the executive pastry chef for Hello Cupcake in Washington, said he was dedicated to simple, natural ingredients. His cakes are made with flour and butter, and his red icing gets its color from strawberry purée. But the sprinkles that top many of his creations have colorings derived from good old petroleum, the source of artificial colorings. And he has no intention of changing that because the natural stuff just isn't as colorful. "I could live without sprinkles, but why would I want to?" he asked. "They're cupcakes. They're supposed to be fun."

TEN

Bisphenol A Should Be Banned

Dianne Feinstein

The United States must ban the use of bisphenol A (BPA) in cans, bottles, sealants, receipts, and other products, argues Senator Dianne Feinstein in the following viewpoint. Feinstein explains that BPA is an endocrine disruptor, which means it negatively affects the body's hormones. Exposure to BPA can wreak havoc on a person's system, making them prone to cancer, diabetes, early puberty, and other disorders, she claims. BPA is particularly dangerous for growing children: It puts them at risk for developing a variety of learning, behavioral, and communicative disorders. Feinstein says that suspected harmful chemicals should be banned without delay; it makes no sense to her to keep a suspicious product on the market until the worst fears about it are proven true. She calls on the federal government to join China, Canada, France, Denmark, and other countries in banning BPA.

Feinstein is a Democrat who has represented California in the United States Senate since 1992.

Dianne Feinstein, "Ban Unsafe Chemical from Baby Bottles and Cups," CNN.com, July 14, 2011. All rights reserved. Reproduced with permission.

L ast month [June 2011] China banned companies from manufacturing, importing or selling baby bottles that contain bisphenol A (BPA), a potentially dangerous chemical routinely added to everyday plastic products. China joins Canada, France, Denmark and the European Union in recognizing that this chemical is linked to a number of harmful health effects like breast cancer, heart disease, obesity, hyperactivity and other disorders. Unfortunately, BPA is still routinely used in hundreds of consumer products sold in the United States.

BPA became widely used in the manufacturing of plastics in the 1950s. Today, in addition to plastics, the chemical is used in countless consumer products, including the lining of canned food containers, cigarette filters, dental sealants, certain medical devices and the coating of the paper on cash register receipts. Recent studies have found that BPA leaches into canned foods—particularly green beans—from the lining of the can.

A Known Endocrine Disruptor

BPA is a known endocrine disruptor, which means it interferes with how hormones work in the body by blocking their normal function. This chemical is so widespread that it has actually been detected in the bodies of 93% of Americans.

While other countries have banned the use of BPA, the United States, driven by the powerful chemical industry, takes the opposite approach: refusing to regulate BPA until there is strong evidence to prove it is unsafe.

Despite a BPA investigation by the Environmental Protection Agency, and other numerous studies, the United States still does not have a nationwide ban of the chemical. Even though BPA has been linked to so many harmful health effects, it is still used in American products—most notably in infant and children's feeding products.

Just this summer [2011], the American Medical Association [AMA] adopted a new policy recognizing that BPA is an endocrine-disrupting chemical and urged a ban on the sale of these products. The AMA also urges the development and use of safe alternatives to BPA for the linings of infant formula cans and other food can linings.

Health Effects of BPA

It wasn't long ago that we didn't have much information about plastics. We could easily pour some milk into a plastic bottle,

US Senator Dianne Feinstein of California supports a ban on the use of bisphenol A (BPA) in products because she believes it negatively affects the body's hormones and makes people more prone to cancer, diabetes, and other disorders.

heat it up in the microwave and not think twice. We now know that when plastic heats up, chemicals leach into the milk and are released into the body when the milk is consumed.

Infants and children, because of their smaller size and stage of development, are particularly at risk from the harmful health effects of BPA. But since BPA is not listed on food or drink labels, we have no way of knowing our daily exposure, or which products to avoid.

In fact, more than 200 studies link BPA exposure to breast and prostate cancer, cardiac disease, diabetes and early puberty.

There is no good reason this country should continue to expose our children to a chemical that is known to disrupt the way our hormones work when there are safe, BPA-free alternatives available for baby bottles, sippy cups, and baby food and infant formula packaging.

Companies and States Taking Action

Companies have begun to phase out BPA. [Petroleum company] Sunoco has said it will refuse to sell the chemical without a guarantee that it will not be used in children's products. Eden Valley Organics now sells beans in BPA-free cans, and Walmart and Toys "R" Us no longer sell baby bottles containing the compound. At least 14 baby bottle manufacturers offer BPA-free alternatives or have banned the use of the chemical.

Eight states have already taken their own measures to ban BPA in some form, and pending the governor's signature, Delaware will become the ninth. Twelve more states (California, Hawaii, Illinois, New Jersey, South Dakota, Kentucky, Maine, Oregon, Pennsylvania, Texas, Tennessee and North Dakota) have considered bills on this issue. This is commendable.

The next step is a change in federal law. A simple first step is to take action to protect the most vulnerable—babies and children—and get this chemical out of baby bottles, sippy cups, infant formula cans and baby food containers.

We must not use our kids as guinea pigs with a chemical that may seriously harm their health. Chemicals should not be used

Bisphenol A (BPA) Is Unsafe

Reports from the consumer advocacy group the environmental working group show that BPA is at unsafe levels in one of every ten servings of canned foods (11 percent) and one of every three cans of infant formula (33 percent).

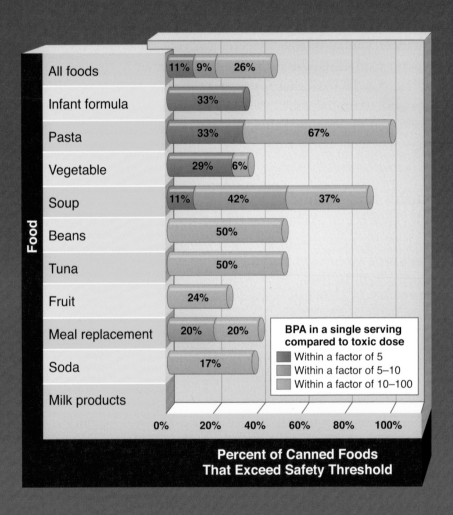

Taken from: Environmental Working Group, 2011.

in food products until they are proven to be safe. I will continue to fight to keep BPA out of the products we use to feed our babies and children, and I've sponsored the Ban Poisonous Additives Act to support the effort.

Until BPA is proven to be absolutely harm-free to our kids, it should be banned from containers used for children. If China can do it, so can we.

ELEVEN

Bisphenol A Should Not Be Banned

Lisa De Pasquale

In the following viewpoint Lisa De Pasquale maintains that there is no reason to ban bisphenol A (BPA). She agrees that BPA is present in detectable levels in many products and in people's bodies, but its mere presence is not anything to fear, she argues. She claims that multiple studies have shown BPA to be safe in the amounts it is present in most peoples' systems—studies that have linked it to diabetes or breast cancer were either poorly conducted or misreported. De Pasquale thinks BPA is another example of how people panic when they lack understanding of a product or are faced with something new. In her opinion, hysteria over BPA is silly and ignorant and potentially more dangerous than BPA itself.

De Pasquale is writer based in Alexandria, Virginia, and the former director of the Conservative Political Action Conference (CPAC). She writes articles from a conservative point of view for publications like *Human Events*.

You can't turn on the local news or look at the magazine aisle in the supermarket without being bombarded with hysterical headlines.

"Killer Celery" (*Good Housekeeping*).

"The Poison That Hid in Our Home" (*Redbook*).

"Dangers Lurking in Your Water Bottle" (KIFI, Wyoming).

"BPA Dangers in Your Pantry?" (ABC News)

In one of my favorite books, *Spin Sisters: How the Women of the Media Sell Unhappiness—and Liberalism—to the Women of America*, author and former magazine editor Myrna Blyth writes about the

A collection of sport and baby bottles that contain bisphenol is seen here. The author argues that BPA should not be banned because it prevents botulism and salmonella contamination and is safe for humans.

The Many Uses of Bisphenol A (BPA)

Bisphenol A continues to be used in large quantities because it has proven to be a cheap and stable way to make a wide variety of much-needed products. It also is a lucrative industry: the five American companies that make BPA—Bayer, Dow, Hexion Specialty Chemicals, SABIC Innovative Plastics (formerly GE Plastics), and Sunoco—bring in more than $6 billion a year from sales of BPA. These are two reasons why legislators are hesitant to ban it.

Common Uses for BPA	
Liners of food cans	Medical devices
Liners of drink cans	Sunglasses
Infant formula cans	CDs and DVDs
Insides of water pipes	Electronic equipment
Dental fillings	Automobile parts
Baby bottles	Sports equipment
Water coolers	Construction glazing
Water bottles	"Bulletproof" glass
Tableware	Receipts
Food storage containers	

Compiled by the editor.

scare tactics used by the media. "Often, a hint of conspiracy is added ('100 Urgent Health Risks Doctors Don't Tell You About') to ratchet up the fear factor and make victims—sometimes just being a woman makes you a victim—even more appealing to readers."

Hysteria over BPA Is Hazardous to Sanity

Lately the "danger du jour" perpetuated by the hysterical, ratings-seeking media is the level of bisphenol A (also known as BPA) found in water bottles, canned foods and even thermal cash-register tape. Are evil corporations poisoning consumers for quick profits?

As with the global warming campaign, the Left and its cohorts in the media have succeeded in ignoring the science and instead ginning up a public frenzy by simply proving that global temperature changes or traces of BPA can be found in your food.

BPA is used in many common plastics and used in an epoxy lining in canned goods to prevent botulism and salmonella contamination. The Left's motive in promoting the bad science of "BPA contamination" is clear: It allows them access to every industry that contains BPA.

BPA Is Safe in Amounts Consumed

BPA alarmists draw attention to the "leaching" (Ooh, scary!) that happens when the lining in canned goods seeps into its contents. In the *National Review*, Julie Gunlock wrote, "To illustrate this leaching, the Breast Cancer Fund sent a selection of canned goods showing BPA had indeed leached into the food. The amount of BPA in the tested foods ranged from a high of 148 to just 10 parts per billion (ppb)."

Gunlock points out that the European Union's allowable amount is 600 parts per billion, and it may even increase to 3,000 parts per billion based on new studies.

Just like rising temperatures don't prove human-caused global warming, the existence of BPA doesn't prove that it actually has harmful effects when ingested.

Flawed Studies, Bad Science

The media has hyped several inherently flawed studies that blame everything from breast cancer to diabetes on BPA. In some of these studies, BPA is injected into the bloodstream of mice at amounts from 10 to 10,000 times the amount humans come in contact with at one time. Additionally, most human interactions with BPA are ingested, not injected into their bloodstream. Numerous studies have found that BPA is metabolized just like everything else and doesn't remain in the body. (See the physiology best seller even liberals can understand, *Everybody Poops*.)

When the Environmental Protection Agency commissioned a study that showed that BPA at normal levels had no harmful effects, it got very little attention. The EPA study, which was also mirrored by the Food and Drug Administration and the Center for Disease Control, showed that there were no discernible traces of BPA after it had metabolized. "In a nutshell," says the author of the study, Justin Teeguarden, "we can now say for the adult human population exposed to even very high dietary levels, blood concentrations of the bioactive form of BPA throughout the day are below our ability to detect them, and orders of magnitude lower than those causing effects in rodents exposed to BPA."

Global Consensus on BPA's Safety

In addition to U.S. agencies determining that BPA is safe, the World Health Organization, Food Standards Australia New Zealand, and European Food Safety Authority have also come to the same conclusion.

Despite numerous global authorities deeming BPA safe, legislatures in California and Connecticut have moved to ban the thermal cash receipts with traces of BPA based on a faulty study by Greenpeace Germany. Because when you think of science without an agenda, you think Greenpeace! Their victory in Connecticut opens the door to more states and more products on their radar.

Panic Makes for Poor Policy

Giving in to junk science to appease the Left's danger du jour is not just about yielding to a nanny state, but also ignores the unintended consequences. There is currently a chemical miracle that allows people to buy convenience food at a reasonable price and prevents botulism and salmonella poisoning. It's BPA.

Bad policy results when you combine media hysteria with political motives. We know that the Left and environmentalists will intentionally mislead the public with junk science. The hysterical media will repeat their talking-points to scare people into not changing the channel.

TWELVE

Consumers Want Products with Natural and Organic Ingredients

Carolyn Dimitri and Catherine Greene

The United States Department of Agriculture (USDA) is responsible for developing US policy on farming, agriculture, and food. In the following viewpoint, Carolyn Dimitri and Catherine Greene, two scientists with the USDA, explain that consumers are increasingly demanding natural and organic products that are made without artificial ingredients. The USDA reports that the growth in demand for organic products has caused a growth in acreage of organic farmlands. The Food Market Institute contends that a large portion of consumers buy organically grown products in order to maintain their health.

Dimitri and Greene are scientists with the USDA's Economic Research Service.

Burgeoning consumer interest in organically grown foods has opened new market opportunities for producers and is leading to a transformation in the organic foods industry. Once a niche product sold in a limited number of retail outlets, organic foods are currently sold in a wide variety of venues including farmers markets, natural product supermarkets, conventional supermarkets, and club stores. Many U.S. manufacturers and distributors are specializing in processing and marketing organic products, while some longtime manufacturers of conventional products have introduced organic items to their product lines. As a result, an ever-widening array of organic agricultural and food products is now available. Since the early 1990s, certified organic acreage has increased as producers strive to meet increasing demand for organic agricultural and food products in the United States. The dramatic growth of the industry spurred Federal policy to facilitate organic product marketing, and is leading to new government activities in research and education on organic farming systems. This report summarizes growth patterns in the U.S. organic sector in recent years, by market category, and describes various research, regulatory, and other ongoing programs on organic agriculture in the U.S. Department of Agriculture. . . .

Consumption Characteristics of the U.S. Organic Sector

A number of academic and industry studies have been conducted to examine consumer behavior and identify their motivation for purchasing organic foods. Many of the industry studies use consumer surveys, which seek to identify how often consumers purchase organic food, their motivations for purchasing organic food, and demographic data on organic food purchasers. University studies have adopted different approaches to assess consumer buying behavior and to identify which characteristics (for example, income, food quality, educational level, concern for the environment, or family size) affect whether consumers will purchase organic food.

Several industry groups have surveyed consumers about their preferences and buying habits for organic food. The results of the different surveys are not always consistent. *The Nutrition Business Journal* reported that 11 percent of consumers purchased some organic food in 2000, and less than 2 percent are regular purchasers. Results of the Hartman Group's 2000 survey suggest that 3 percent of consumers regularly buy organic products. The Walnut

Organic Sales Grow Every Year

Concern about artificial ingredients has helped drive sales of organic food and beverages, which increase every year.

Year	Category	
	Organic Food	Growth
2000	6,100	21.00%
2001	7,360	20.70%
2002	8,635	17.30%
2003	10,381	20.20%
2004	12,002	15.60%
2005	14,223	18.50%
2006	17,221	21.10%
2007	20,410	18.50%
2008	23,607	15.70%
2009	24,803	5.10%
2010	26,700	7.7%

Organic as % of Total Food: 4%

Taken from: Organic Trade Association and the Center for Economic Vitality.

Acres Survey (2001) found that 63 percent of respondents purchased organic food at least sometimes, and 57 percent of the purchasers had been doing so for at least 3 years. The Food Marketing Institute's survey (2001) found that 66 percent of surveyed shoppers bought organically grown foods.

In 2001, the Food Marketing Institute's survey indicated that 37 percent of shoppers said they purchased organically grown food to maintain their health; and 44 percent of these shoppers

Organic foods are sold in 83 percent of retail food stores, and the existence of nearly twenty thousand natural food stores in the United States testifies to the increased consumer demand for organic products.

had purchased organic food in the past 6 months. Consumers surveyed by the Hartman Group (2000) gave the following reasons for purchasing organic food: health and nutrition (66 percent), taste (38 percent), environment (26 percent), and availability (16 percent). The Fresh Trends (2001) survey revealed that 12 percent of the shoppers surveyed reported that whether a product is organic is a primary factor in their purchasing decision. Sixty-three percent of the respondents of the Walnut Acres Survey believed that organic food and beverages were better for them and were more healthful than their conventional counterparts. Fresh Trends (1996, 1998, 2000, 2002) found little difference between the purchasing habits of men and women.

Over the years, Fresh Trends found that, of the shoppers that had purchased organic produce in the previous 6 months, more purchased vegetables than fruit (according to the 1996 survey, 24 percent purchased fruit and 84 percent purchased vegetables; according to the 2000 survey, 35 percent purchased vegetables). Apples and tomatoes led the list of fruit and vegetables purchased by the shoppers surveyed by Fresh Trends. According to the Hartman Survey (2000), the top 10 organic products purchased were strawberries, lettuce, carrots, other fresh fruit, broccoli, apples, other fresh vegetables, grapes, bananas, and potatoes. The Hartman survey also suggested that fruits and vegetables were "gateway categories" (typically the first organic products purchased by consumers). The Walnut Acres Survey (2002) indicated that 68 percent of consumers revealed that price is the main reason they did not purchase organic food.

Academic researchers have taken a slightly different tack in studying organic consumers by complementing surveys with statistical analysis to depict the typical consumer. Some studies reveal conflicting results, most likely because of the different methodological approaches. Consumers considered the following factors important when purchasing fresh produce: price, size and packaging, whether the item is on sale, and whether the item is organic. Age, gender, and having a college degree had little impact on a shopper's decision to buy organic produce. Consumers with higher incomes and higher levels of education are willing to pay more for organic potatoes, while consumers with advanced degrees are less likely to buy organic produce. Appearance of fresh produce mattered, and the larger the number of cosmetic defects, the less likely would an organic product be purchased.

One picture of the typical organic shopper is a younger household in which females do the shopping; smaller and higher income households are the most likely purchasers of organic produce and organic apples. Households knowledgeable about alternative agriculture are more likely to purchase organic produce and those concerned about the environment are more likely to purchase organic apples. Those concerned about food safety are more likely to buy organic produce and organic apples. Those who enjoy trying new products are more likely to purchase organic produce. Households with children under 18 are more likely to purchase organic produce and organic apples. Consumers with children are willing to pay less for organic potatoes and more likely than other households to purchase organic apples.

Strategies to increase purchases of organic food include shelf-labeling, which had a mixed effect on sales in an upscale grocery store but a significantly positive effect on sales of dairy products, pasta, bread, cereal, and carrots in a discount retailer in the Minneapolis and St. Paul markets.

The recent addition of organic food sales to scanner data, by AC [Nielsen] and Information Resources, Inc., has made possible econometric studies of consumer demand for organic food. Frozen organic vegetables, organic milk, and organic baby food all exhibited high price elasticity of demand, meaning that the quantity purchased responds greatly to price changes (that is, quantity purchased increases by more than 1 percent when prices fall by 1 percent). For some frozen vegetables, there was little crossover between purchases of organic and conventional products, so that changes in prices of either commodity had no significant impact on quantities purchased. For other products (milk and baby food), the conventional and organic products are substitutes, so that increases in the price of the conventional product result in consumers' purchasing a greater quantity of the organic products. . . .

THIRTEEN

Consumers May Not Want Alternatives to Artificial Ingredients

Taryn Luna

In the following viewpoint, Taryn Luna discusses how the sales of Necco wafer candies plummeted after the company switched to all-natural ingredients. Necco wafers previously included artificial ingredients and colorings, but given the popularity of all-natural ingredients, it switched to using beet juice, red cabbage, cocoa, and cinnamon to sweeten its candies. Customer reaction was swift and harsh: The new versions of the candies were widely rejected. Luna uses the example of Necco wafers to show how alternatives to artificial ingredients are not always adequate when consumers want food to look and taste the way they expect it to.

Luna is a reporter for the *Pittsburgh Post-Gazette*.

New England Confectionery Co. thought it could make its old-fashioned wafer appeal to a modern, health-conscious consumer by coloring and flavoring it with all natural ingredients such as cabbage and beets. Instead, sales of Necco Wafers fell 35 percent. "There were stacks and stacks of letters and e-mails that said, 'Why did you do this? You ruined it,'" recalled Steve Ornell, Necco's vice president of sales.

The All-Natural Flop

Less than two years after going all natural, the Revere company has gone back to its original recipe in hopes of recouping lost sales and loyal fans of the 164-year-old candy. The chalky, sugary candy that comes in eight colors is once again made of artificial dyes and flavors.

Steve Almond, the Boston author of *Candyfreak: A Journey Through the Chocolate Underbelly of America*, which includes a chapter on Necco, said the disastrous debut shouldn't have come as a surprise. "For kids, it's about bright colors and lots of sugar, not about healthy options," he said. "And even when it comes to adults, candy remains a childish pleasure. There's a big nostalgia element here, as well. If you loved Neccos as an old-time candy, the idea of an updated version feels wrong."

In 2009 the New England Confectionary Company began using natural ingredients like cabbage and beets to flavor and color their Necco candy wafers. After two years of slumping sales, however, the company decided to resume the use of artificial ingredients.

Consumers Want the Colors and Tastes They Love

Just ask lifelong fan Jackie Bowden, owner of Billy Boy Candies in New Bedford [Massachusetts]. "The colors were bland. The taste was bland," said Bowden, 66, who stopped eating the all-natural wafers. "My theory is that if it wasn't broken, it shouldn't have been fixed. They proved it." Bowden is also a distributor of Necco Wafers to other retailers, and the switch, she said, hurt every aspect of her business. "Once people started trying it, they weren't buying anymore," she said. "There were no repeat sales, and customers said it was lousy. No one was happy."

Michael F. Jacobson, executive director of the Center for Science in the Public Interest, which advocates for legislation that eliminates artificial dyes in all US food products, said companies like Necco would have more support in switching to natural products if there were legislation to back them. "The unfortunate experience indicates the need for national action," he said. "People's perceptions would change if artificial coloring were removed from all foods."

One Candy's Successful History

The Necco Wafer dates back to 1847 when English immigrant Oliver Chase invented the lozenge cutter enabling him to make the candies. The cutter is believed to be the first American candy machine, and Union soldiers during the Civil War carried the candies, then known as "hub wafers," according to Necco.

In 1901, Chase merged his business with two other companies to form the New England Confectionery Co., and about a decade later the wafers adopted the "Necco" name.

During World War II, sales of the wafers peaked when the US government ordered the company to produce the candy for American troops overseas. When servicemen returned home, they continued to buy up the chalky treats.

Starting in the 1980s, Necco began forming an old-fashioned candy empire, scooping up competitors that produced Candy House Buttons, Mary Jane, Haviland Chocolates, and Clark Bar.

Despite the acquisitions—and the fact that Necco produces more than eight billion Sweetheart Conversation Hearts every year for Valentine's Day—the company still views the wafers as its core product. Necco, privately held, wouldn't disclose annual sales for the company, but Chicago research firm SymphonyIRI Group reports that all Necco candy brands generated $38.9 million in sales at many US retailers in 2010.

The Switch to Natural Ingredients

Necco went all-natural with its wafers based on a recommendation from its marketing division and focus groups. Some of the ingredients in the wafers' artificial dyes like Yellow 5 and Red 40 have come under fire after studies linked them to hyperactivity in children and to cancer-causing agents. The company also consulted with some retail outlets before the all-natural product hit the market; they supported the change.

The new formula took all of 90 days to create. Necco traded artificial flavors and dyes for more expensive natural flavors and colors derived from red beet juice, purple cabbage, cocoa powder, paprika, and turmeric.

The wafers traditionally have come in eight flavors—orange, lemon, lime, clove, chocolate, cinnamon, licorice, and wintergreen. But the company couldn't make the all-natural color of lime match the original so it was dropped from the lineup. The white wafer already used all-natural coloring and went unchanged.

Only four of the seven flavors needed to be altered to go all-natural. In most cases, the company used a mixture of natural and artificial flavors to make the wafers, so to go all-natural meant removing the artificial flavor. For example, chocolate was made entirely of cocoa extract and cinnamon went to all-natural cinnamon.

Jeff Green, Necco's vice president of innovation, who designed the new product, said the taste difference between the original and all-natural wafer was nearly undetectable. The difference lies in the wafers' pale new colors. That, he believes, is what went wrong. "The perception started with their eyes and affected their tongues," Green said.

AH! DEHYDROGENATED NON-MILK FAT SOLIDS WITH A SOUPCON OF DEOXYHYDROPESANE AND SWEETENERS ...JUST LIKE MUM USED TO MAKE

"Ah! Dehydrogenated non-milk fat solids with a soupcon of deoxyhydropesane and sweeteners . . . just like mum used to make," cartoon by Fran. www.CartoonStock.com.

People Do Not Want Change

Necco has gone all-natural with other candies without much fanfare. For example, Clark Bars now use real peanut butter and chocolate. Raspberry and orange flavor versions of Thin Mints now use all-natural ingredients.

But Necco found that its wafer customers were different, and after more than a year of dramatic sales decline, officials owned up to their mistake. Over the summer, the company brought back the original formula, making the all-natural wafer history. It will take about a year for the transition to be complete as retailers sell out of their stock of all-natural wafers.

"What we found out from people was that they like the product," Green said of Necco wafers, "and they don't want change."

What You Should Know About Artificial Ingredients

New York City became the first city to ban restaurants from using partially hydrogenated oils, or trans fats, in December 2006.

California became the first state to ban restaurants from using partially hydrogenated oils, or trans fats, in 2008.

Denmark banned trans fats in 2003.

Puerto Rico banned trans fats in 2007.

Switzerland banned trans fats in 2008.

Restaurants have been banned from using trans fats in Philadelphia; Boston; Cambridge, MA; and Stamford, CT; as well as in Montgomery County, MD; Brookline County, MA; King County, WA; and Nassau, Westchester, Suffolk, Albany, and Broome Counties in New York.

Opinions About Artificial Ingredients

In 2012, *Food Safety* magazine reported that

- 43 percent of consumers feel unfavorably about processed foods;
- most consumers—76 percent—associate processed foods with artificial colors and flavors;

- 68 percent associate processed foods with chemicals that have long names;
- only one in three Americans agrees that food colors positively add to the appearance of foods;
- just over half of consumers know that both natural and artificial food colors must be labeled on food packages;
- nearly 50 percent of consumers agree that food colors must be reviewed and approved by the US government before being added to food products;
- food and beverage purchase decisions are driven largely by taste: 87 percent of consumers rank taste as an important factor while making choices about what to purchase;
- nearly half of all consumers say they look at the ingredients list on food packaging when making food and beverage choices;
- consumers primarily look for food components such as sodium, type of fat, or oil, and sugars while less than half—44 percent—of consumers who look at ingredients lists say they look for artificial ingredients;
- about 21 percent of consumers look for food colors on ingredients labels; and
- about 18 percent of consumers are concerned with being able to pronounce the ingredient names listed on labels.

The 2011 International Food Information Council (IFIC) Foundation Food & Health Survey reported the following changes in consumer behavior regarding artificial sweeteners:
- In 2011, fewer consumers (29 percent) agreed that low-calorie sweeteners can play a role in weight loss or weight management, or can be part of an overall healthful diet (24 percent) than in 2010, when 38 percent and 29 percent thought so, respectively.
- In 2011, an increased percentage of Americans (34 percent) reported a lack of knowledge about low-calorie sweeteners compared with previous years (27 percent in 2010).

A 2010 poll taken jointly by Harris Interactive and the Sugar Association found the following opinions of artificial ingredients:

- Although the majority of parents with children under eighteen say they believe all natural products are better for them than those containing artificial ingredients, a minority was able to recognize common artificial sweeteners used in everyday foods and beverages.
- Eighty-seven percent of parents say the sweetener used in a product is at least somewhat important to them when deciding what food or beverages to serve their kids.
- Eighty-one percent of parents said natural foods are better for them than those with artificial ingredients.
- More than half (52 percent) of all parents make an effort to avoid artificial sweeteners.
- Even though about three-quarters (76 percent) of parents turn to food labels to help guide purchases, fewer are actually able to identify common artificial sweeteners used in food products.
- When shown the ingredient label of a popular children's product, given to dehydrated infants, only 4 percent of parents could identify all the sweeteners.
- About one in 7 (13 percent) parents could not identify any of the four sweeteners used.
- Only 1 percent of parents had ever heard of the artificial sweetener neotame.
- Only 5 percent of parents had ever heard of the artificial sweetener acesulfame-K.
- Only 5 percent of parents had ever heard of the artificial sweetener erythritol.
- Only 14 percent of parents had ever heard of the artificial sweetener polydextrose.
- While branded chemical artificial sweeteners—Equal (90 percent), Sweet'N Low (90 percent), and Splenda (87 percent)—had high name recognition, those figures dropped by as much as about half when the scientific names of these products often found on food labels were used, such as aspartame (67 percent), saccharin (73 percent), and sucralose (43 percent), respectively.

What You Should Do About Artificial Ingredients

Why Do We Use Artificial Ingredients?

Artificial ingredients are used because many people like the convenience and versatility they offer food products. In general, artificial ingredients help maintain or improve a food's safety and freshness, helping products stay on the shelf longer. They also help foods stay clear of dangerous toxins, molds, or bacteria. Other artificial ingredients improve a food's taste or appearance by affecting its "mouth feel" or texture. Still others affect a food's nutritional value, allowing it to have more vitamins and minerals, or fewer calories and less fat, than it would naturally.

If you are curious or concerned about artificial ingredients, educate yourself about what they do and in which foods they are found. Information below, provided by the Food and Drug Administration, can help you. In general, there are a few different categories of artificial ingredients: those that make foods taste better or make tasty foods less fattening, those that improve the food's shelf life, and those that make the food appear more appetizing.

In What Foods Are Artificial Ingredients Found?

Modern chemistry has allowed people to indulge their love of sweet and fatty foods without ingesting as many calories as they would if they ate their natural counterparts. Artificial sweeteners are popular because they add sweetness without extra calories. The most common artificial sweeteners include sorbitol, mannitol, corn syrup, high fructose corn syrup, saccharin, aspartame, sucralose, acesulfame potassium (acesulfame-K), and neotame. These sweeteners are commonly found in beverages, baked goods, confections, sugar substitutes, and many other processed and diet foods.

Similarly, fat replacers chemically synthesize a food's texture, but without using actual fat like butter or oil. Reduced-fat foods are very popular, and chemicals like Olestra, cellulose gel, carrageenan, polydextrose, modified food starch, microparticulated egg white protein, guar gum, xanthan gum, and whey protein concentrate are found in baked goods, dressings, frozen desserts, confections, cake and dessert mixes, and dairy products.

Yet another group of artificial ingredients that affect the way food tastes includes flavor enhancers, like monosodium glutamate (MSG), hydrolyzed soy protein, autolyzed yeast extract, disodium guanylate or inosinate. These enhance flavors already present in foods (without providing their own separate flavor) and are found in processed foods that aim to mimic the flavor of something else.

A different class of artificial ingredients, called preservatives, helps products stay fresh and safe. Ascorbic acid, citric acid, sodium benzoate, calcium propionate, sodium erythorbate, sodium nitrite, calcium sorbate, potassium sorbate, BHA, BHT, EDTA, and tocopherols are found in fruit sauces and jellies, beverages, baked goods, cured meats, oils and margarines, cereals, dressings, snack foods, and even fruits and vegetables. They prevent food from spoiling by being overtaken by bacteria, molds, fungi, or yeasts. They also chemically slow or prevent changes in color, flavor, or texture, and stave off rancidity. Similarly, lactic acid, citric acid, ammonium hydroxide, and sodium carbonate are pH-control agents that control acidity and prevent foods from spoiling; they are found in beverages, frozen desserts, chocolate, low-acid canned foods, and baking powder.

Some artificial ingredients are intended to make a food look more appetizing. This is the purpose of food dyes, some of the most controversial artificial ingredients on the market. Artificial food dyes include FD&C Blue nos. 1 and 2, FD&C Green no. 3, FD&C Red nos. 3 and 40, FD&C Yellow nos. 5 and 6, Orange B, and Citrus Red no. 2, while natural ones include annatto extract; beta-carotene; grapeskin extract; cochineal extract, or carmine; paprika oleoresin; caramel; fruit and vegetable juices; and the spices turmeric and saffron. Both artificial and natural food dyes help prevent discoloring due to exposure to light, air, moisture, or temperature. They also help foods look "how they are supposed to look" to consumers. Artificial food colorings are found in many processed foods you would expect, such as candies, snack foods, margarine, cheese, soft drinks, jams and jellies, gelatins, pudding and pie fillings, juices, sodas, processed macaroni and cheese, and thousands of others.

Another group of artificial ingredients affects the way foods look and feel. Emulsifiers help foods mix smoothly and prevent ingredients' separation over time or while in packaging. Soy lecithin, mono- and diglycerides, egg yolks, polysorbates, and sorbitan monostearate are emulsifiers found in salad dressings, peanut butter, chocolate, margarine, and frozen desserts and help keep products stable, reduce stickiness, control crystallization, and keep ingredients dispersed and dissolvable.

Also affecting foods' look and feel is a class of chemicals called stabilizers, thickeners, binders, and texturizers. Substances like gelatin, pectin, guar gum, carrageenan, xanthan gum, and whey are often added to frozen desserts, dairy products, cakes, pudding and gelatin mixes, dressings, jams and jellies, and sauces. Similarly, anticaking agents help keep powdered foods powdery, or other dry foods dry, by preventing them from absorbing moisture. For this reason, calcium silicate, iron ammonium citrate, and silicon dioxide are found in salt, baking powder, confectioner's sugar, and other powdery substances. The opposite of anticaking agents are humectants, which help products retain moisture. Glycerin and sorbitol are used for this purpose and are found in products like shredded coconut, marshmallows, soft candies, and confections.

Some of these chemicals raise more controversy than others. Although all have been approved for use by the FDA and require no additional labeling by law, groups like the Center for Science in the Public Interest report that many of the above are toxic and should be avoided. Specifically, CSPI says that people should avoid ingesting any food that contains: acesulfame-k; artificial colorings Blue no. 2, Green no. 3, Orange B, Red no. 3, Yellow no.

5 and Yellow no. 6; aspartame; butylated hydroxyanisole (BHA); caramel coloring; Olestra; partially hydrogenated vegetable oil; potassium bromate; propyl gallate; saccharin; and sodium nitrate and nitrite. They warn people to exercise caution with artificial colorings Blue no. 1, Citrus Red no. 2, Red no. 40, brominated vegetable oil (BVO), butylated hydroxytoluene (BHT), diacetyl, heptyl paraben, and stevia. Use the articles and other resources in this book to do more research on which artificial ingredients you feel comfortable consuming, and make sure you can express clear and evidenced reasons why.

Actions to Take

Now that you are familiar with the categories and names of artificial ingredients, you are in a good position to recognize them and can start reading product labels. Get in the habit of scanning nutritional labels for the above ingredients. Go through the products in your family's kitchen. How many products contain artificial ingredients, and what kinds? Keep a list or make a chart of how many times or in how many products Red no. 40 or Olestra are used, for example.

You can see how products differ in their use of artificial ingredients: now it is time to taste that difference. Save up, or ask your parents for, some money so you can conduct an experiment. Go to the store and buy two versions of products to taste test. You might, for example, purchase a box of mass-produced macaroni and cheese (which has artificial ingredients) and also a box of organic macaroni and cheese (which does not). Or, you can look for two different kinds of chips, juice, pasta sauce, soup—there are countless products to taste test. (You might need to make a trip to a natural or organic market to find a larger selection of artificial-ingredient-free products, though many brands are now carried at chain grocery stores).

Whatever kind of food you settle on, prepare both, and compare the difference. Does one taste better than the other? Does one taste more like what you expect that type of food to taste like? Do they differ in color or texture? Is one saltier or sweeter, or does one leave a stronger aftertaste? Enlist your friends or family in the experiment, and take notes. Do the majority of your tasters express a clear preference for one product over another? Are taste preferences evident across demographic groups—for example, do younger people tend to prefer the foods with natural ingredients or artificial ingredients?

Now that you have tasted for yourself the difference between foods with and without artificial ingredients, decide whether you want to keep such products in your house. Ask to accompany a parent to the grocery store, or volunteer to do a portion of the family grocery shopping yourself. Make an effort to identify brands, products, or items that have a level of artificial ingredients that you are comfortable consuming. Compare the prices of foods high in artificial ingredients with ones that are low in artificial ingredients. What trends do you notice? Are foods low in artificial ingredients more expensive, less expensive, or cost about the same? Are there differences in packaging, logos, or marketing in these products? Teach the members of your family what you have learned about artificial ingredients, and enlist their help in changing the foods your family buys.

Another place to take action is your school's own cafeteria. Does your school serve hot lunches? Cold lunches? What kinds of ingredients go into making these dishes? Are there vending machines available, and do students largely rely on them for food? Request a meeting with a representative from the food and beverage service or an administrator familiar with the cafeteria program to go over why your school serves the kinds of food it does. Are such foods cheaper? Do they have a longer shelf life? If you are really motivated about the issue, you could write an article about the issue for your school paper or post about it in a blog for a journalism or humanities class. If you find that the food offered by your school is overly high in artificial ingredients, you could circulate a petition to deal with the problem. Once you collect a significant number of signatures, submit it to school administrators and begin discussions about changing the menu. No matter what action you decide to take, be sure you are highly informed on the issue and can defend whatever position you decide to take.

The editors have compiled the following list of organizations concerned with the issues debated in this book. The descriptions are derived from materials provided by the organizations. All have publications or information available for interested readers. The list was compiled on the date of publication of the present volume; names, addresses, phone and fax numbers, and e-mail and Internet addresses may change. Be aware that many organizations take several weeks or longer to respond to inquiries, so allow as much time as possible.

American Council on Science and Health (ACSH)
1995 Broadway, 2nd Fl.,
New York, NY 10023-5860
(212) 362-7044
e-mail: acsh@acsh.org • website: www.acsh.org

ACSH provides consumers with scientific evaluations of food and the environment, pointing out both health hazards and benefits. It participates in a variety of government and media events, from congressional hearings to popular magazines.

Cato Institute
1000 Massachusetts Ave. NW
Washington, DC 20001-5403
(202) 842-0200 • fax: (202) 842-3490
e-mail: cato@cato.org • website: www.cato.org

The institute is a libertarian public policy research foundation dedicated to limiting the role of government and protecting individual liberties. It asserts that the concern over the possible health risks of many artificial ingredients and other chemicals is overstated and believes that government should not interfere in the choices people make about what they eat. The institute publishes the quarterly *Cato Journal*, the bimonthly *Cato Policy Report*, and numerous books and commentaries.

Center for Food Safety (CFS)
660 Pennsylvania Ave. SE, Ste. 302
Washington, DC 20003
(202) 547-9359
website: www.centerforfoodsafety.org

The CFS is a nonprofit public interest and environmental advocacy group. It challenges harmful food-production technologies and promotes sustainable alternatives. Its website contains a wealth of information about artificial ingredients, food safety, genetically engineered food, cloned food, and other topics related to food safety.

Center for Science in the Public Interest (CSPI)
1220 L St. NW, Ste. 300
Washington, DC 20005
(202) 332-9110
e-mail: cspi@cspinet.org • website: www.cspinet.org

CSPI is a nonprofit education and advocacy organization committed to improving the safety and nutritional quality of the US food supply. It publishes a multitude of reports on the dangers of artificial ingredients such as aspartame, bisphenol A (BPA), high fructose corn syrup, food dyes, and other additives.

Environmental Protection Agency (EPA)
Ariel Rios Bldg.
1200 Pennsylvania Ave. NW
Washington, DC 20460
(202) 272-0167
website: www.epa.gov

The EPA is a government agency that regulates pesticides under two major federal statutes. It establishes maximum legally permissible levels for artificial ingredients and pesticides in food, registers certain food chemicals for use in the United States, and prescribes labeling and other regulatory requirements to prevent unreasonable adverse effects on health or the environment.

Environmental Working Group
1436 U St. NW, Ste. 100
Washington, DC 20009
(202) 667-6982
website: www.ewg.org

This nonprofit consumer advocacy group seeks to protect public health and the environment. It aims to protect the most vulnerable segments of the human population—children, babies, and infants in the womb—from health problems from toxic contaminants and artificial ingredients. It publishes numerous reports, fact sheets, and briefs about the safety of many artificial ingredients.

Food and Drug Administration (FDA)
10903 New Hampshire Ave.
Silver Spring, MD 20903
(888) INFO-FDA (463-6332)
website: www.fda.gov

The FDA is a public health agency, charged with protecting American consumers by enforcing the federal Food, Drug, and Cosmetic Act and several related public health laws. To carry out this mandate of consumer protection, FDA has investigators and inspectors cover the country's almost ninety-five thousand FDA-regulated businesses. Its publications include government documents, reports, fact sheets, and press announcements about many topics, including an array of artificial ingredients and other food additives.

Food First Institute for Food and Development Policy
398 Sixtieth St., Oakland, CA 94618
(510) 654-4400
website: www.foodfirst.org

Food First, founded by Frances Moore Lappé, the author of *Diet for a Small Planet*, promotes sustainable agriculture. Its current projects include the Cuban Organic Agriculture Exchange Program and Californians for Pesticide Reform.

Natural Resources Defense Council (NRDC)
40 W. Twentieth St.
New York, NY 10011
(212) 727-2700 • fax: (212) 727-1773
e-mail: nrdcinfo@nrdc.org • website: www.nrdc.org

Founded in 1970, the NRDC actively works to curb global warming, promote clean energy alternatives, defend endangered wildlife and wild places, prevent pollution, and revive the world's oceans by ending overfishing, creating marine protected areas, and improving ocean governance. The organization also investigates the use of artificial ingredients and whether certain food additives should bear special labels.

Organic Consumers Association
6771 S. Silver Hill Dr.
Finland, MN 55603
(218) 226-4164
website: www.organicconsumers.org

The Organic Consumers Association promotes the growth of organic and sustainable agricultural practices. Its activist strategies include education, boycotts, grassroots lobbying, litigation, networking, direct-action protests, and media events. Its website features an entire section of articles on food safety and artificial ingredients.

Organic Trade Association (OTA)
28 Vernon St., Ste. 413
Brattleboro, VT 05301
website: www.ota.com

The Organic Trade Association is a membership-based business association that focuses on the organic business community in

North America. OTA's mission is to promote and protect the growth of organic trade to benefit the environment, farmers, the public and the economy.

Rodale Institute
611 Siegfriedale Rd.
Kutztown, PA 19530-9320
(610) 683-1400
e-mail: info@rodaleinst.org • website: www.rodaleinstitute.org

The Rodale Institute was founded in 1947 by organic pioneer J.I. Rodale. The institute employs soil scientists and a cooperating network of researchers who document how organic farming techniques offer the best solution to global warming and famine. Its website offers information on the longest-running US study comparing organic and conventional farming techniques, which is the basis for Rodale's practical training to thousands of farmers in Africa, Asia, and the Americas.

United States Department of Agriculture (USDA)
1400 Independence Ave. SW
Washington, DC 20250
website: www.usda.gov

This government organization is charged with regulating the standards for any farm, wild crop harvesting, or handling operation that wants to sell an agricultural product as organically produced. The USDA has set requirements for the importing and exporting of organic products. More information about this process is available on its website, as are numerous fact sheets and publications about the state of food in America.

BIBLIOGRAPHY

Books

Carl F. Cranor, *Legally Poisoned: How the Law Puts Us at Risk from Toxicants*. Cambridge, MA: Harvard University Press, 2011.

Jon Entine, *Scared to Death: How Chemophobia Threatens Public Health*. New York: American Council on Science & Health, 2011.

Victoria Inness-Brown, *My Aspartame Experiment: Report from a Private Citizen*. Jamul, CA: Writers Without Borders, 2010.

Richard J. Johnson and Timothy Gower, *The Sugar Fix: The High-Fructose Fallout That Is Making You Fat and Sick*. New York: Gallery Books, 2009.

Joseph Mercola and Kendra Degen Pearsall, *Sweet Deception: Why Splenda, NutraSweet, and the FDA May Be Hazardous to Your Health*. Corning, CA: Nelson Books, 2006.

Marion Nestle, *Food Politics: How the Food Industry Influences Nutrition and Health*. Berkeley: University of California Press, 2007.

———, *Safe Food: The Politics of Food Safety*. Berkeley: University of California Press, 2010.

Bill Statham, *What's in Your Food? The Truth About Additives from Aspartame to Xanthan Gum*. Philadelphia: Running Press, 2007.

Periodicals and Internet Sources

Trevor Butterworth, "Breast Cancer Fund's Scary Thanksgiving Study Is a Turkey," *Forbes*, November 16, 2011. www.forbes.com/sites/trevorbutterworth/2011/11/16/breast-cancer-fund-scary-thanksgiving-study-is-a-turkey.

Bill Chappell, "Customer Outrage Forces Necco to Put Artificial Ingredients Back into Wafers," *Salt* (blog), National Public Radio, October 26, 2011. www.npr.org/blogs/thesalt

/2011/10/26/141732915/customer-outrage-forces-necco-to-put
-artificial-ingredients-back-into-wafers.

Elena Conis, "Saccharin's Mostly Sweet Following," *Los Angeles Times*, December 27, 2010. http://articles.latimes.com/2010 /dec/27/health/la-he-nutrition-lab-saccharin-20101227.

Julie Deardoff, "Do Synthetic Food Colors Cause Hyperactivity?," *Chicago Tribune*, January 1, 2011. http://articles.chicagotribune. com/2011-01-01/health/ct-met-food-dyes-20110101_1_food -dyes-food-colors-food-ingredients.

Dina ElBoghdady, "Study Links BPA Exposure in Wombs to Behavior Problems in Toddler Girls," *Washington Post*, October 24, 2011. www.washingtonpost.com/business/economy/study -links-bpa-exposure-in-womb-to-behavior-problems-in-toddler -girls/2011/10/24/gIQA6ihRDM_story.html.

Mike Esterl, "Can This Chip Be Saved? Frito-Lay Chips Go All-Natural, Ditching Artificial Ingredients," *Wall Street Journal*, March 24, 2011. http://online.wsj.com/article/SB1000142405 2748704050204576218492608111416.html.

Amanda Gardner, "FDA Weighs Food Dye, Hyperactivity Link," CNN.com, March 30, 2011. www.cnn.com/2011 /HEALTH/03/30/fda.food.dye.health/index.html.

Julie Gunlock, "Chemical Warfare," *National Review*, September 26, 2011. www.nationalreview.com/home-front/278409/chemical -warfare/julie-gunlock.

Jeffrey Kluger, "Why a Smart Tax on Soda Would Work," *Time*, December 6, 2011. http://healthland.time.com/2011/12/06/why -a-smart-tax-on-soda-would-work.

Nicholas Kristof, "Chemicals in Our Food, and Bodies," *New York Times*, November 8, 2009. www.nytimes.com/2009/11/08 /opinion/08kristof.html.

Lyndsey Layton, "Food Dyes' Favor Fades as Possible Links to Hyperactivity Emerge," *Washington Post*, March 24, 2011. www .washingtonpost.com/politics/food-dyes-favor-fades-as-possible -links-to-hyperactivity-emerge/2011/03/24/AFmAhoYB_story .html.

Chuck Norris, "'Natural' Flavor: Not So Natural," World Net Daily, July 29, 2011. www.wnd.com/index.php?pageId=327625.

Barack Obama, "Toward a 21st Century Regulatory System," *Wall Street Journal*, January 18, 2011. http://online.wsj.com/article /SB10001424052748703396604576088272112103698.html.

David Penberthy, "Mmm & mmm. The Nanny State Can't Have My Smarties," *Punch* (Australia), November 22, 2011. www .thepunch.com.au/articles/mmm-mmm.-the-nanny-state-cant -have-my-smarties.

Caitlin Rose, "Obesity in America," Down to Earth, September 16, 2011. www.downtoearth.org/health/nutrition/obesity-america.

Cynthia Sass, "The Truth About High-Fructose Corn Syrup," *Shape*, n.d. www.shape.com/healthy-eating/diet-tips/truth-about -high-fructose-corn-syrup.

Michael D. Shaw, "It's Time to End the Anti-BPA Hysteria," *Health News Digest*, November 23, 2009. www.gasdetection.com /news2/health_news_digest235.html.

Aviva Shen, "How Do 'Natural' Non-sugar Sweeteners Stack Up? Faddy Foods," *Salon*, March 24, 2011. www.salon.com /2011/03/24/natural_sweeteners/.

Melanie Warner, "Why 'Natural' Is One of the Most Meaningless Words in Food Packaging," CBS News, May 5, 2010. www.cbsnews.com/8301-505123_162-44040714 /why-natural-is-one-of-the-most-meaningless-words-in-food -packaging/?tag=bnetdomain.

Carly Weeks, "Natural Deli Meats May Not Be as Healthy as You Think," *Globe and Mail* (Toronto), February 6, 2012. http://m .theglobeandmail.com/life/health/new-health/health-nutrition /nutrition-features/natural-deli-meats-may-not-be-as-healthy-as -you-think/article2201790/?service=mobile.

Todd Wyn, "The ABCs of Environmental Hysteria: Activists, Bisphenol-A and Children," Cascade Policy Institute, April 26, 2011. http://cascadepolicy.org/pdf/pub/4-26-11ToddEnviron mental%20HysteriaPDF.pdf.

Qing Yang, "Gain Weight by 'Going Diet?' Artificial Sweeteners and the Neurobiology of Sugar Cravings," *Yale Journal of Biology and Medicine*, June 2010. www.ncbi.nlm.nih.gov/pmc/articles /PMC2892765.

Websites

Be Food Smart (www.befoodsmart.com) This website has a searchable database of hundreds of artificial ingredients. Users can input an ingredient to see in which foods it commonly appears, as well as other information about it.

CornSugar (www.cornsugar.com) This site, sponsored by the Corn Refiners Association, an industry organization, presents a positive view of high-fructose corn syrup.

Natural Ingredient Resource Center (www.naturalingredient. org) This site, which supports the labeling of foods that contain artificial ingredients, offers articles and other resources about artificial ingredients.

Natural News (www.naturalnews.com) This site offers a clearinghouse of articles, briefs, news, and press releases on artificial ingredients, sweeteners, food dyes, and other food industry topics.

Sweet Misery: A Poisoned World (http://topdocumentaryfilms .com/sweet-misery-a-poisoned-world) Readers can watch a full-length documentary about the dangers of aspartame on this site.

Tox Town (http://toxtown.nlm.nih.gov/index.php) This government-sponsored site offers a wealth of reliable information about toxic chemicals in the environment, including information on bisphenol A (BPA), phthalates, and other substances.

AAP (American Academy of Pediatrics), 10

AC Nielsen and Information Resources, Inc., 86

Acceptable daily intake (ADI)
of aspartame, 20, 22

ActionOnAdditives.com (website), 56

Almond, Steve, 88

AMA (American Medical Association), 71

American Academy of Pediatrics (AAP), 10

American Medical Association (AMA), 71

Artificial ingredients
ability of parents to identify, 30

banned, 15

cause behavioral problems in children, 46–51

consumers exaggerate health threat of, 17–24

global sales of, by region, 44

link between behavioral problems and, is unproven, 52–57

percentage of packaged food containing, 5

pose a serious health threat, 10–16

safety of, is difficult to determine, 41–45

taking personal action to avoid, 45

Artificial sweeteners
are very dangerous, 32–40

are very safe, 25–31

high-intensity, 27

Aspartame, 18, 23, 35
acceptable daily intake of, 20, 22

biological systems affected by, 37

deceptive marketing of, 33

FDA's assessment of, 42

health problems associated with, 33–34, 36–38

is safe, 21–22

metabolism of, 19

Aspartic acid, 18, 19, 37

August, Jason, 16

Ban Poisonous Additives Act (proposed), 75

Behavioral problems
in children, artificial ingredients cause, 46–51

difficulty in proving link between food dyes and, 42–43

link with artificial ingredients is unproven, 52–57

Benzidine, 60, 61
Berman, Richard, 8
Bisphenol A (BPA), 11
  baby bottle containing, 77
  common uses of, 78
  as endocrine disrupter,
    43–44, 71–72
  health problems linked to, 13
  percentage of canned foods
    with, 74
  should be banned, 70–75
  should not be banned, 76–80
Blyth, Myrna, 77–78
Bowden, Jackie, 89
BPA. See Bisphenol A
Brown, Jerry, 44

California, bans bisphenol A
  in baby bottles, 44
Candyfreak (Almond), 88
Carcinogenicity
  difficulty in determining,
    59–60
  FDA testing for, 60–62
CDC (Centers for Disease
  Control and Prevention), 6,
  13
Center for Science in the
  Public Interest, 8, 58, 69
Centers for Disease Control
  and Prevention (CDC), 6,
  13
Chase, Oliver, 89
Consumers
  exaggerate health threat of
    artificial ingredients, 17–24

  may not want alternatives to
    artificial ingredients,
    87–91
  surveys on organic food
    purchasing by, 82–86
  want products with natural/
    organic ingredients, 81–86
Cosmetics/personal care
  products, 15–16
  dyes in, 48, 59, 62

De Pasquale, Lisa, 76
Delaney amendment (1960),
  63
Department of Agriculture,
  US (USDA), 5
Depression, aspartame-based
  products and, 29–30, 37
Diet Supplement Health and
  Education Act (DSHEA,
  1994), 22
Dimitri, Carolyn, 81
Dopamine, 29, 37
DSHEA (Diet Supplement
  Health and Education Act,
  1994), 22

EFSA (European Food
  Standards Agency), 55
Environmental Protection
  Agency (EPA), 80
European Food Safety
  Authority, 22
European Food Standards
  Agency (EFSA), 55
Excitotoxins, 37

FDA. *See* Food and Drug Administration, US
FD&C dyes
adverse reactions to, 19
Red No. 2, 13
Yellow No. 6, 67
Feingold, Benjamin, 48
Feinstein, Dianne, 70, 72
Food, Drug, and Cosmetic Act (1938), 62, 63, 64
Food and Drug Administration, US (FDA), 8, 11, 20, 42
constraints on delistings by, 64–65
food dyes certified by, in 2009, 69
review of research on food colorings, 47
testing for carcinogenicity by, 60–62
Food colorings/dyes, artificial, 61
certified by FDA in 2009, 54
daily per capita marketing of, 65
difficulty in proving link between behavioral problems and, 42–43
endanger children, 47
natural alternatives to, 39, 64
should be banned, 58–65
should not be banned, 66–69
Food Marketing Institute, 83–84

Food Standards Agency (FSA, UK), 43, 53
Formaldehyde, 18, 19, 37
Formic acid, 18, 19
Fresh Trends, 84–85
Fructose, 24, 38–39
See also High fructose corn syrup
FSA (Food Standards Agency, UK), 43, 53

GAO (US Government Accountability Office), 11
Generally regarded as safe (GRAS) designation, 11
Government Accountability Office, US (GAO), 11
GRAS (generally regarded as safe) designation, 11
Green, Jeff, 90, 91
Greene, Catherine, 81
Gunlock, Julie, 79

Hall, Harriet, 17
Hansen, Michael, 11, 14
Harris, Gardiner, 66
Hartman Group, 82, 84, 85
Health problems, associated with
aspartame, 33–34, 36–38
bisphenol A, 13, 73
High fructose corn syrup (HFCS), 5–6, 24, 39
Hu, Frank, 5–6
Hutton, Deirdre, 56–57

ILSI (International Life Sciences Institute), 24
Ingredient lists, 7
Inness-Brown, Victoria, 38
Insulin, 18–19, 40
International Life Sciences Institute (ILSI), 24

Jacobson, Michael F., 46, 89
Johnston, Rob, 52
Journal of Food Science, 12
Journal of Industrial and Engineering Chemistry, 62

Krebs, John, 56

Lancet (journal), 53
L'Oreal, 16
Luna, Taryn, 87

Martini, Betty, 21
Mercola, Joseph, 21, 32
Meridian Tapping Technique (MTT), 38
Methanol, 18, 19, 37
Miller, Todd, 69
Mission Possible World Health International, 21
MTT (Meridian Tapping Technique), 38

National Institutes of Health (NIH), 27
National Review (magazine), 79
Necco Wafers, 64, 87–88, 88

history of, 89–90
switch to natural ingredients in, 90–91
Nestlé, 16
Nestle, Marion, 41, 68
New England Confectionery Co., 87
New England Journal of Medicine, 22
New York City, ban on trans fats in, 7
NIH (National Institutes of Health), 27
Nutrition Business Journal, 82

Obesity epidemic, annual cost of, 50
Organic foods, growth in sales of, 83
Ornell, Steve, 87

Packaged food
artificial ingredients common in, 13–14
labeling of trans fats in, 7
percentage with artificial ingredients, 5
Parabens, 14, 15
Personal care products. *See* Cosmetics/personal care products
Pesticides, 44
Phenylalanine, 18, 19, 37
Phenylketonuria (PKU), 24
Phthalates, 14, 15
PKU (phenylketonuria), 24

Polyoxyethylene (20) sorbitan monostearate, 13
Public Health Law Center, 6, 7

Ramazzini Foundation, 22
Roberts, Susan B., 25

Saccharine, 42
San Francisco Chronicle (newspaper), 41
Schab, David W., 46
Serotonin, 37
Shelke, Kantha, 68
Sodium benzoate, 54
Sodium cyclamate, 13
Spin Sisters (Blyth), 77–78
Stevenson, Jim, 53, 54, 55–56
Stevia, 18, 22–23, 40, 98
Surveys
  on labeling artificial colors in food, 63
  on organic food purchases, 82–86
  of parents on ability to identify artificial ingredients, 30
Sweet Deception (Mercola), 37

Teeguarden, Justin, 80
Toxic Substances Control Act (1976), 10
Toxicology Science (journal), 12
Trans fats, 5, 6
  average US consumption of, 7–8

USDA (US Department of Agriculture), 5

Wakefield, Andrew, 53
Walnut Acres Survey, 82–83, 84
Wansink, Brian, 67
Wartman, Kristen, 10
Washington Post (newspaper), 5
Weight/weight loss
  artificial sweeteners are important for, 28–31
  diet foods/drinks cause problems with, 34–36
Weiss, Ted, 62
Why Your Child Is Hyperactive (Feingold), 48

Yellow 5, 60, 61